SECRETS OF PATERNITY

SUSAN CROSBY

Silhouette® Desire

Published by Silhouette Books

America's Publisher of Contemporary Romance

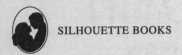 **SILHOUETTE BOOKS**

ISBN 0-373-76659-9

SECRETS OF PATERNITY

Copyright © 2005 by Susan Bova Crosby

Visit Silhouette Books at www.eHarlequin.com

Printed in U.S.A.

"You Intrigue Me," James Said.

She did? She was so straightforward, usually, and so…*un*intriguing. Was it because she was keeping herself mysterious, and therefore, hard to get? "Then I should keep doing what I'm doing," she said leisurely.

"Ah. It's the chase that excites you."

Caryn stared to flirt back, then realized she had no right to. What was she thinking? She gathered up her long-denied, flattered libido and adjusted her body language and tone of voice. "How do I get home from here?"

He barely skipped a beat before giving her directions, then took a step back. His smile disappeared.

"I'll see you in a couple of days," she told him.

He nodded.

She felt awful as she pulled away, like a big tease, like a teenager without any life skills. She'd responded to him without thinking it through. She was sinking deeper into a situation she should be avoiding at all costs.

And she was afraid she wasn't going to be able to stop.

Dear Reader,

Thank you for choosing Silhouette Desire, where this month we have six fabulous novels for you to enjoy. We start things off with *Estate Affair* by Sara Orwig, the latest installment of the continuing DYNASTIES: THE ASHTONS series. In this upstairs/downstairs-themed story, the Ashtons' maid falls for an Ashton son and all sorts of scandal follows. And in Maureen Child's *Whatever Reilly Wants…*, the second title in the THREE-WAY WAGER series, a sexy marine gets an unexpected surprise when he falls for his suddenly transformed gal pal.

Susan Crosby concludes her BEHIND CLOSED DOORS series with *Secrets of Paternity*. The secret baby in this book just happens to be eighteen years old…. Hmm, there's quite the story behind that revelation. The wonderful Emilie Rose presents *Scandalous Passion,* a sultry tale of a woman desperate to get back some steamy photos from her past lover. Of course, he has a price for returning those pictures, but it's not money he's after. *The Sultan's Bed,* by Laura Wright, continues the tales of her sheikh heroes with an enigmatic male who is searching for his missing sister and finds a startling attraction to her lovely neighbor. And finally, what was supposed to be just an elevator ride turns into a very passionate encounter, in *Blame It on the Blackout* by Heidi Betts.

Sit back and enjoy all of the smart, sensual stories Silhouette Desire has to offer.

Happy reading,

Melissa Jeglinski

Melissa Jeglinski
Senior Editor
Silhouette Desire

Please address questions and book requests to:
Silhouette Reader Service
U.S.: 3010 Walden Ave., P.O. Box 1325, Buffalo, NY 14269
Canadian: P.O. Box 609, Fort Erie, Ont. L2A 5X3

SUSAN CROSBY

believes in the value of setting goals, but also in the magic of making wishes. A longtime reader of romance novels, Susan earned a B.A. in English while raising her sons. She lives in the central valley of California, the land of wine grapes, asparagus and almonds. Her checkered past includes jobs as a synchronized swimming instructor, personnel interviewer at a toy factory and trucking company manager, but her current occupation as a writer is her all-time favorite.

Susan enjoys writing about people who take a chance on love, sometimes against all odds. She loves warm, strong heroes, good-hearted, self-reliant heroines…and happy endings.

Susan loves to hear from readers. You can visit her at her Web site, www.susancrosby.com.

For those who've loved and lost, and somehow carry on,
especially Bobbie, Judy, Patt and Ruth.

One

Caryn Brenley waited until dark before staking out the beautiful home in San Francisco's upscale Forest Hill area. She might be a rank amateur at such intrigues, but two things she did know: first, she had a better chance of seeing someone arrive home on a weeknight after five o'clock than before it, and second, night provided better cover for someone to sit in a car and observe unnoticed. This late in October, with the switch back to standard time, night came early.

She didn't have to wait long before a silver van pulled up to the residence she was watching from across the street and down a few houses. The garage door opened and the van disappeared inside. Caryn clenched her steering wheel. Would the driver have to come outside and go up the stairs, or was there access from the garage to inside the house?

Her question was answered quickly when two children,

a boy about eight and a girl about five, emerged from the garage followed by a tall, slender woman in a black business suit.

He was married. With children.

It changed everything.

Before the woman and children went into the house, a Mercedes pulled up beside them. The kids jumped up and down and waved. The woman smiled. Again the garage door opened—

A motorcycle pulled up behind Caryn's Explorer. In her rearview mirror she saw a man in full biker gear climb off the bike and head to the nearest house, the one in front of which Caryn was hiding in plain sight. He grabbed the contents of the mailbox and jogged up the stairs.

She went back to watching the family greet each other, but she focused on the man in the business suit who'd just arrived across the street. Husband. Father. He wasn't as tall as she would have imagined, although his hair was dark, as she expected. There was no way of checking out his eye color from where she sat, and his dark suit and overcoat didn't show his physique well.

Now what? She'd come to satisfy her curiosity, to see him for herself. But short of marching up and asking his name, she couldn't know for sure that he was James Paladin, her son's biological father.

Maybe she should leave well enough alone—

No. As appealing as that sounded, she couldn't. Paul made a promise nineteen years ago. He could no longer keep that promise, but he would expect her to. She expected it of *herself*. That's why she was here, skulking like the amateur sleuth she was.

The family went into their house together, the man carrying the little girl, her arms wrapped around his neck. She gave him repeated kisses on his cheek.

The fire went out of Caryn. There had to be a more subtle way to get her answers than confronting the man to verify that he was James Paladin—someplace away from his family. Then when she knew for sure, she would tell Kevin. The choice had to be his, a tough decision for an eighteen-year-old, especially one who'd been to hell and back in the past year.

She drummed her fingers on her steering wheel as she considered possibilities, then decided to go home and come up with a solution for another day. Maybe she could come back in the morning, follow him to his work and see if there was a way to determine his identity there. She would have to call in sick, herself. Lose a day's wages and tips, something she couldn't afford to do.

Resigned, Caryn started her engine, shifted into Reverse and released the emergency brake just before she spotted the biker hurrying back down the steps. He looked straight at her. She grabbed the map from the seat beside her and buried her face in it, not wanting him to get too close a look, in case she had to stake out James Paladin again.

She heard his motorcycle rev but kept her map raised, waiting for him to pull away first. His engine cut out, then a sharp knock on her window startled her, panicked her.

The map went flying. Her foot slipped off the brake. The Explorer rolled backward.

"What the—? Stop!" He banged on the hood. "Hit the—"

She jammed on the brakes. Metal hit metal. Then came silence. Hot, heavy, condemning silence.

Even through her closed window she could hear him

swearing, succinctly, menacingly. Her heart thundered, deadening his words.

What had she done? She'd never had an accident. Never had a ticket. And the one time she needed to blend with the surroundings—

She stopped the thought. Took a breath. Then she shoved the jumbled map aside and looked out her window at him. Okay, she thought as her heart thumped a little slower and her hearing returned. Okay. What was done, was done. While she stared at the man, he ripped off his helmet and tunneled his fingers through his dark hair. Eyes, green and direct, drilled her. The angles of his face sharpened beneath a several-days' growth of dark beard.

She rolled down the window and tried to smile.

Given the driver's reckless behavior, he expected a teenager. Instead the idiot who'd just creamed the fender of his two-month-old, custom-detailed Screamin' Eagle Harley—which he'd just gotten out of the shop from a previous accident—was a woman, one closer to his own age of forty-two. He cataloged her, as he always did with people at first meetings: auburn hair, straight, chin length and with bangs. Slender and small boned. He couldn't judge her height precisely, but average or a little taller. Hesitation hovered in her blue eyes as she said hello, her inflection turning the single word into a question.

He rested his fists against the top of her window frame, not trusting himself not to yell at her and turn her into a quivering mass of contrition. Terrorizing wasn't his style—most of the time, anyway—but, damn, he'd waited almost a year for that bike. A year. And this was the second time in a month he'd been hit.

Finally he gave her a "stay-put" look and went to assess the damage. Fender bent straight into his tire, just like the last time.

He grabbed a notepad and pen from the saddlebag, copied down the woman's license plate number, then stared at the asphalt until he was calm enough to talk to her.

"I'm so sorry," she said as he approached.

He met her gaze. Turquoise eyes, he noted, not blue. And she wore red lipstick. He hated red lipstick.

"You startled me when you banged on my window. My foot slipped—"

"I knocked," he said, correcting her. "Not even loudly." So much for being a Good Samaritan. He'd seen the map and thought she was lost.

He flipped open his notepad to an empty page. "Your tailgate is dented, by the way."

"Bad?"

"You can see for yourself."

She didn't budge. Was she afraid to get out of the car? He looked that intimidating?

"We need to exchange insurance information," he said.

After a few seconds her body language changed, not in a sexual way but a casual can-we-be-friends pose—except she looked too nervous for it to be real. What was going on?

"Could we just keep this between us," she said, "instead of involving the insurance companies? I'll pay cash for the repairs."

Ah. Afraid of being canceled by her insurance company—or maybe having her license pulled? Should he sanction her game by going along with her? Or would the world be better off without her on the road?

While he debated how to answer her, he peered into her

SUV. Spotless. Not a single scrap of paper or water bottle or straw wrapper. She wore a white blouse and black knee-length skirt, like a waitress's uniform. Not the serial-accident type, at least not at first impression. So, what was her story? A husband who wouldn't tolerate another accident?

He dropped his gaze to her left hand. No ring. As he looked, she touched her thumb to the vacant spot, as if a ring was still there.

He'd made her wait long enough, he decided. And his silence hadn't made her tip her hand, anyway. He admired that—grudgingly. He widened his stance and crossed his arms. "You want to pay cash, it's fine with me."

Her shoulders dropped, her relief palpable. "How much do you think it will cost?" she asked.

He shoved the notepad and pen toward her. "Why don't you put down your name, address and phone number. I'll send you the bill."

He knew by her expression she wouldn't write down anything, even though she poised the pen above the paper. After a few seconds, she angled the tip away.

"Could you get an estimate over the phone now?" she asked.

"Doubtful." He didn't know why he was stringing her along. He knew the answer, probably to the penny, if the damage was what it had been the last time. He was just reluctant to let her go. Maybe it was the way she wouldn't back down even though he seemed to terrify her.

"Can you try?"

He was entertained by her discomfort. She obviously wasn't used to intrigue or she would've realized he could track her down through her license plate, whether she gave him her name or not.

He unzipped his jacket, pulled out his cell phone and pressed a button until the right number appeared on the screen. The phone rang twelve times before it was answered. "Yo, Bronco," James said. "It's Paladin."

Her face paled. She busied herself with closing the pad of paper, as if the task was huge, aligning the edges of the tablet precisely, one side then the other, her fingers shaking. He figured he should just tell her what he did for a living—that she didn't have to be afraid of him.

"Jamey! How's that baby runnin'?"

"Could be better. There's been an accident—" He held the phone away as Bronco shouted a few choice words. From her wince, James figured the Harley wrecker had heard them, too.

"Some woman driver hit you?" Bronco asked when he ran out of steam.

"As a matter of fact." He was glad the woman in question couldn't hear the sexist statement.

One more curse blasted the airwaves. "What's the damage?"

"Same as before."

"Drivable?"

"Not until it's fixed."

"I'll come take a look in a while," he said with a sigh.

He turned his back on the woman responsible and massaged his forehead. "Got a loaner?" he asked quietly.

"You on a job?"

"Yeah."

"I can scrounge up something. Won't be an Eagle. It'll have some muscle, though."

"Works for me. Thanks. I'll see you later." He snapped the phone shut and tucked it in his pocket before he turned back to face the woman and gave her an amount. "That's if there's no structural damage."

She swallowed. "Plus you won't have it as transportation."

"Right."

She looked at his house as if assessing his net worth. She also seemed to have calmed down. "You don't have a car?" she asked.

"That's not the point."

A small fire flared in her eyes. "Look, I'm not denying my responsibility. I'm sorry you'll be inconvenienced. I'll go to the bank right now and bring the cash back to you, then I'll stop by again in a few days to see if there are further costs. Will that be okay?"

"No."

She gave him a long, cool look, which interested him as much as the heated one had.

"You said you were okay with my paying cash."

"I am. But I'm going with you to the bank." James wasn't about to let her out of his sight yet. He wasn't worried about finding her again, since he had her license plate number, but, well, frankly, she intrigued him—from her red lipstick, to her ringless finger that she continued to use as a touchstone, to her modest skirt and blouse.

"I don't give rides to strangers."

Implied in her tone was the fact he looked like part of a biker gang, which was his job at the moment—but she wouldn't know that unless he chose to tell her. Not yet, he decided.

"You're welcome to follow me," she said primly.

He almost laughed. Damn, she was cute with her hackles up. "You won't give me the slip?"

She went rigid. "I keep my word."

He'd already figured that out, which is why he found it mystifying that she wouldn't give him her name and phone number, at least, if not her address and insurance information. She was a contradiction. He liked contradictions.

"I'll get my car out of the garage and follow you," he said, backing away. "Don't leave without me."

"You'd better hurry. They close in twenty minutes."

James deliberately chose his BMW convertible instead of the Taurus he kept for surveillance work. Okay, so he was grandstanding a little. He liked the contradiction he was showing her, as well.

Think I'm some kind of gang member, do you? Someone to be afraid to give your phone number to? Well, here's another side of me. What would you have done if you'd hit the BMW instead, and I'd been wearing a suit and tie, and was clean shaven?

Knowing the answer—or figuring he did—he followed her up the street, uncharacteristically enjoying the fact she was nervous around him, he who usually made the effort to put people at ease.

A little intrigue. Maybe it was just what he needed while he waited to hear from the child he'd never met.

Somehow Caryn had prevented herself from hyperventilating. Had she written down his address wrong? She couldn't imagine making that kind of mistake, but how else could she have been watching the house across the street? The wrong house.

On top of that confusion, however, James Paladin was a puzzle, she thought as she pulled into the parking lot of her bank. A contradiction. A…big problem, frankly. Obviously he was a risk taker, like her late husband, Paul. And a man used to taking charge and giving orders, also Paul's MO. Paul had ridden a motorcycle—and he'd died in an accident on the bike he cherished a year ago.

She was beginning to see why Paul had chosen James to provide the sperm for Caryn's artificial insemination almost nineteen years ago. She'd never met him, had only learned of his existence last week, and now they were about to turn each others' lives upside down. And Kevin's.

Was he married? Did he have children? She hadn't noticed a wedding ring on his finger, but he also seemed the type to shun public displays of, well, possession, for lack of a better word. He seemed…unpossessable.

She parked the car and turned off the engine, saw him pull in a few spaces away. She wished she could tell him who she was, what their connection was. She couldn't. If Kevin decided he didn't want to meet the man responsible for his existence, it was his choice, as per a written agreement between Paul and James made all those years ago. Caryn had found it only last week while cleaning out the paperwork she'd dumped from Paul's desk into boxes for her move back to San Francisco. Then she'd discovered a letter James had sent last year with his current address— the wrong address, apparently—and his phone number, nothing more.

That note had been mailed a week before Paul's death to a private mailbox of Paul's that Caryn hadn't known existed. That hurt still lingered. How many other secrets had he kept that she hadn't uncovered yet?

As for the potential relationship between James and her son, she couldn't intrude. Kevin alone held that key.

She didn't know whether she wanted James in her life or not. Everything was finally settling down for her. She'd been prepared to have Kevin's biological father become part of *his* life—*assumed* that he wanted to be part of Kevin's life—but that was before she met the man, when he'd been just words on paper, not a flesh-and-blood person. A man in full biker regalia. A man who made her hormones come out of a long hibernation.

He came up beside her, his sheer size in his boots and leathers making her feel like a background singer to a rock star.

"You don't need to go inside with me," she said.

"I have nothing else to do."

She met his innocent gaze. Up close he was even more attractive, his eyes a lighter green than she'd first thought, his hair not just dark brown but thick and shiny. Only the scruffy beard detracted.

"I won't walk up to the teller with you," he added.

He seemed to be enjoying the moment. She didn't know why she thought that, because he wasn't smiling, but something lurked in his eyes, some sense of mischief at the absurdity of what they were doing. Cloak-and-dagger stuff. She smiled. She couldn't help it. Oh, the irony. The first man she'd been even the slightest bit attracted to since Paul died, and he happened to be…well, who he was.

"What's so funny?" he asked, as they entered the bank just before closing.

The security guard locked the door behind them then stood at his post, letting each person out as they finished their business.

"Just in the nick of time," she said.

"That's funny?"

She shrugged. *Let him wonder.*

He lingered a distance away as she withdrew a huge chunk of her savings and asked the teller for an envelope to put the money in, which she then passed to James. The guard gave him the once-over, his gaze shifting from James to Caryn and back, as if trying to match them as a couple— or perhaps trying to determine if James had coerced her into giving him money.

She smiled at the guard. He unlocked the door to let them through, bade them a good night. James walked with her to her car.

"I'll need a receipt," she said to him.

He pulled his pad of paper from his pocket, scrawled something on it, signed it, ripped it off the wire spiral and presented it to her. "How about taking me to my mechanic's shop in the morning to pick up my loaner?"

"You have no friends?"

"Of course I have friends."

She studied him. Mischief was back in his eyes. "Take a cab," she said. "Add the fare to my bill."

He grinned. She felt her face heat and tried to draw his attention from the fact. "I'm gathering that this wasn't the first accident you had with your bike."

He cocked his head. "It's the second, and very similar."

"Seems to me you should learn to park your bike differently."

He laughed, then after a brief hesitation he reached into the inside pocket of his jacket and pulled out a business card, passing it to her. "I'll see you in a few days, Ms.... Mysterious."

He walked away. She looked at his card. James Paladin, Investigator, ARC Security & Investigations.

Well. Maybe he wasn't like Paul, after all.

Two

An hour later Caryn was holding her breath as she waited for her son to say something. Anything.

"I don't want to meet him," Kevin muttered at last.

He pushed away from the kitchen table and stalked to the window overlooking their tiny backyard. Caryn sat quietly, giving him time to let the idea of James Paladin settle. She'd had a week's advantage on him in that regard, but she was by no means calm or accepting, either.

She'd explained everything she knew—that Paul had chosen James specifically as the sperm donor, that they'd entered into a written agreement which stated that the resulting child, if there was one, would have the right to contact James upon turning eighteen. She told Kevin how she'd found the agreement in Paul's paperwork, then about the other letter giving James's current contact information. That was it. Bare bones information. No note saying he still wanted to meet Kevin. No hint at all. Name, correct address—she'd double-checked that—and phone number. Period.

"I don't have to see him," Kevin added, his arms crossed, his tone harsh. "The agreement says so."

"That's right. Nothing requires you to."

He shoved his hands through his hair, as James had done earlier. The gesture caught her by surprise. Maybe Kevin had always done that, but it took on more significance now—heredity, not environment.

"I wish you hadn't told me," he said, firing a look at her.

"I wish I hadn't had to."

His hesitation lasted several beats. "'Never make a promise you can't keep, and always keep your promises,'" he said, parroting a lifetime of her own words to him.

It wasn't only her philosophy but Paul's, as well. She'd fulfilled her end of the bargain. Now she was free of the technical part of her responsibility. She still had to deal with the results of backing into his Harley—plus if Kevin did at some point decide to meet him, the emotional aspects of the whole business.

She stood, smoothed the wrinkles from her skirt. Her fingertips brushed against the outline of the business card in her pocket. "He's a private investigator, by the way," she said, giving him the last piece of information, one she thought might interest him too much.

Kevin lifted his head. "Yeah?"

"Will you tell me if you decide to meet him?" she asked, wishing she could hug him as though he were five years old again and make everything better. He'd had a horrible time adjusting to Paul's death.

"I guess so."

"You want to stay for dinner?" she asked.

"Nah. Jeremy's coming over to study. He's bringing pizza."

"Okay." Caryn had bought an old duplex near Kevin's college. They each had their own two-bedroom unit, his downstairs.

"How'd work go?" he asked.

"Good tips today."

"Was Venus there?"

"Yes." She grabbed a glass from the cupboard, turning away from him, keeping her frown to herself. Kevin's crush on the young waitress who worked with Caryn worried her. He didn't need another obsession in his life, and Venus was fast becoming one.

"Did she…say anything about me?"

"No." Caryn kept her voice upbeat and didn't ask questions.

"Okay." He started to leave but stopped, his hand on the doorknob. "What does he—" He frowned. "Do I look like him?"

She nodded. The similarities struck her anew. The same facial features, except eye color. And their hands—long fingers and broad palms. Close in height, too, although James had a man's body, while Kevin was still growing into his.

"Why did Dad choose this guy?"

"I don't know. I gather they knew each other, but I don't know what the connection was."

"Okay." He banged his open hand against the doorjamb. "Later."

After the front door shut she tried to find something mindless to do. She opened the refrigerator, stared inside it, then shut the door. She'd lost weight since Paul died, pounds she hadn't needed to lose. She should fix herself a meal, but she doubted she could eat more than a bite, anyway.

She walked across the slightly warped hardwood floor to where a portable phone hung on the charger base. She picked up the handset. After a minute she carefully returned it to the base. Who could she call? No one. Not until Kevin made a decision to acknowledge James. Until then she couldn't tell her mother, her brother or even her best friend.

She'd had such hope for this move back to her hometown. Some people thought she was clinging to Kevin, that she'd bought the duplex in order to keep him close instead of turning him loose as an independent adult. Maybe that was partly true. He'd had an even harder time than she had adjusting to Paul's death, yet he'd decided to attend Paul's alma mater, to major in criminal justice, like his father.

She worried that Paul's life philosophy was embedded in Kevin, that he would take as many risks, revel in them, actually. He already had the notion that the accident that ended Paul's life was intentional, even though law enforcement people from more than one agency had been involved in the investigation, and nothing they found indicated any hint of truth to Kevin's claim.

Lately Caryn had been wondering the same thing, if not worse.

She took a sip of water, letting go of her worries about Paul and focused on Kevin instead. She'd listened as friends and family advised her to let go of him, that it was time for him to spread his wings—and she'd ignored the advice, because she knew her son better than anyone else did, and she knew he wasn't ready to be cut loose yet. When he was, she would know. She hoped it would be soon, for both their sakes.

For now, however, her longtime curiosity about the man whose generosity had given her Kevin had been satisfied. He was tall, dark and handsome, and her son clearly resembled him. And the man was capable of keeping his temper under control, as witnessed by his demeanor toward her after she'd run into his bike. He was in a profession that required intelligence, cunning, quick-on-his-feet reaction—and a willingness to take risks, the part of Paul she'd had the hardest time dealing with through the years. With good reason, as she'd discovered.

Had Kevin also wondered about the man? She and Paul had never kept it secret that Kevin had been conceived by artificial insemination. But then, Paul had never mentioned James Paladin and the agreement. She understood, perhaps, why Paul had kept it from Kevin, but why hadn't he told her? If she hadn't found the letter of agreement, what would've happened? Would James have found Kevin and her instead, and accused them of not biding by the agreement?

If Kevin didn't contact the man within a certain amount of time, would he come looking? It wouldn't be too difficult for a competent private investigator to find out where they lived.

Maybe she would have to intervene, after all, if only to say that Kevin didn't want contact yet.

But she would give Kevin some time first. Just a little time. She hoped James would, too.

That same evening, James's doorbell rang. His gut clenched as he hurried downstairs and to the front door. Even after a twenty-year career dominated by anticipation, he was surprised at the almost staggering sense of expectation that surged through him every time the phone rang or someone came to the door. But then, this wasn't work related.

"I come bearing food," Cassie Miranda said as she shouldered her way past him, trailing a scent of basil and garlic.

He masked his disappointment—or relief, he wasn't sure—that an eighteen-year-old with maybe his own green eyes wasn't standing there instead. He wished he knew whether he was waiting for a boy or girl. "Did we have plans, Cass?"

She looked around. "Do you have company?"

"No."

"Heath is in Seattle. I got lonely."

He shut the door and followed her to the kitchen. "You've been engaged for three weeks and you've forgotten how to eat alone?"

"Amazing, isn't it?"

James knew why Cassie was there, and it had nothing to do with her fiancé being out of town. In the almost-year that James and Cassie had worked as investigators at ARC Security & Investigations, they, along with their boss, Quinn Gerard, had forged a friendship rare for such independent souls. They were the only people he'd told about what was happening in his life, what he was waiting for.

"Any word?" she asked as she pulled plates from his cupboard.

"Nothing."

"Give them time." Her long, golden-brown braid swung along her lower back as she reached for a couple of wineglasses.

He grabbed a bottle of Merlot. "Maybe Paul decided to ignore our agreement."

"From everything you've told me about Paul Brenley, I don't think you need to worry about him going back on his word." Cassie stopped dishing up the food and set her hands on the counter, leaning toward him. "Let's focus on your biggest worry—what if the kid doesn't want to meet you?"

He plunked down a tub of grated parmesan cheese next to the plates. "Yeah, so? That's normal."

"My point exactly, Jamey. And if you don't hear from them, you only have to track down the Brenley family and get the answers yourself. An easy thing for you, unless they're in witness protection or something." She flashed him a teasing smile then went back to serving generous portions of ravioli. "In fact, I can't believe you haven't tried."

"I agreed to no contact, and I've stuck by it. I don't want to take advantage of my resources unless I have to. We're jaded enough from this business, Cass. Maybe my agreement with Paul was only slightly more than a handshake, but I want to believe he would honor it." Like the Harley wrecker this afternoon, he thought. He wasn't going to track her down, but let her prove him right—that most people were trustworthy.

"Speaking of being jaded," she said, "how was your date last night?"

He'd put the woman out of his mind already. Not very complimentary, he supposed, but he didn't date for fun anymore. Every woman was a potential wife and mother, now that he was looking to settle down. "It was okay," he said.

"How old was this one?"

He gave her a cool look.

"That young, huh?" she asked innocently.

"Need I remind you that your fiancé is eleven years older than you."

"Yeah. Eleven. Not twenty."

"My date wasn't that young."

"How old?"

"Twenty-five."

"Oh, okay. Only seventeen years' difference. Jamey, Jamey, Jamey. I know dating a P.I. can make a woman starry-eyed for some odd reason, but, really, what do you want with someone that young?"

Babies, he thought. A home. "Energy," he said instead with a grin, to which Cassie heaved a huge sigh.

James made it through the evening without telling Cassie about his incident that afternoon with the Harley wrecker, knowing he wasn't ready to deal with Cass's potential interrogation, even though she would like the fact the woman was closer to his own age. *Is she attractive?* Cass would ask. Yes, and although she looked as if a strong wind could blow her away, her personality wasn't subtle. He thought about the empty place on her ring finger. Divorced? Widowed? While there was a certain vulnerability to her, he hadn't seen weakness.

Is she smart? Oh, yeah. He'd especially liked how she'd told him to take a cab and add the cost to her bill.

But the question he was likely avoiding most from Cassie: *What is she hiding?* That he didn't know, but it seemed tied more to her not giving him her name than insurance issues.

The encounter had jarred his life—in a good way—at a time he needed jarring.

After Cassie left around ten o'clock, James sat down at his computer, found he couldn't concentrate, and so he wandered into his backyard. The size of his house and the denseness of foliage blocked most of the street noise and city sounds. The birds slept. A year ago he couldn't have pictured himself living in a place like this, a four-bedroom, stately manor house with room for a family. While he'd been born and raised in San Francisco, and the city had continued to be home base during his twenty years as a bounty hunter, he'd lived in a small, cheap apartment when he wasn't out of town—since his divorce, anyway.

When his father died last year and James decided he'd had enough of life on the road, he'd looked at high-rise condos and lofts, but this house had lured him with unspoken promise, even the yard. This summer he'd planted a small vegetable garden. Next year he would do more. The yard was a work in progress.

As was his life. Gone were the days of tracking down fugitives, at least on a daily basis. He'd signed on with ARC because investigation was what he knew, and even though he still worked more than forty-hour weeks, the clientele had gone way upscale.

He wanted a personal life-change, as well. Home and hearth, although maybe not in the traditional sense. He wouldn't mind if the woman came with children already, except that he would like to have one of his own, too, if it wasn't too late.

One of his own. He had one of his own. He just hadn't had a hand in raising that one. But maybe they could have a relationship, anyway. A friendship. Extended family. Would Paul encourage that? And his wife, Caryn, whom James had never met—would she feel threatened by James's intrusion into their lives? Had they found a way to provide a sibling or two for the first child?

There were plenty of times he'd questioned whether meeting the child was a good idea, given the potential complications to everyone involved, but James would never break his word, never go back on a promise.

It was the lack of control that was hardest for him. He had no control whatsoever.

All he could do was wait.

Three

In a family-friendly neighborhood like his, James expected a lot of trick-or-treaters, but the sheer numbers amazed him. Time after time he answered the door, dropped candy into a paper bag or plastic pumpkin or pillowcase, shut the door and started to walk away, only to hear the bell ring again.

He gave up trying to do anything but give out candy, deciding to sit on his front steps, about four up from the bottom. It was already dark but still early in the evening, a magical time when the littlest kids were brought around by parents who either coaxed them to approach or dragged them away because they were too talkative and curious.

James enjoyed them all. It was his first Halloween in his home, in a real neighborhood, for more years than he could remember. The costumes ranged from store-bought to homemade to thrown together. Pirates swaggered, princesses pirouetted. Some things never changed.

The trick-or-treaters got older as the hour grew later, kids traveling in groups but without adult supervision. They more or less grunted, shoved their bags into range, grunted again then kept going. When the crowds thinned to one or two kids every five minutes or so, he decided to go inside. He stood just as a young man approached and stopped at the bottom of the stairs.

"No costume, no candy," James said lightly. The kid hadn't bothered to don a hat or even carry a prop, unless he considered his black leather jacket and sunglasses, two hours after sunset, a costume.

"I'm Kevin," the boy said, stuffing his hands in his pockets. "Kevin Brenley. Are you James Paladin?"

It was a blow to the abdomen—pain and joy jumbled together, wreaking havoc. Kevin. He had a son. Kevin. How had he doubted for a second that he wanted to meet the boy?

He found his voice. "Yes, I'm James." Their connection was purely biological, but he was there, looking scared and slightly hostile and handsome. James put out his hand. "Thank you for coming."

The boy hesitated a few seconds, shook his hand, then jammed his own back in his pocket.

James tamped down his inner turbulence. "Would you like to come inside?" he asked. He'd faced an escaped murderer with less uncertainty about what to do next.

"Can we just sit here?"

"Sure." James gestured to the spot beside him, resisted smiling when Kevin sat on the step above, as far away as he could get. Damn. What did you say to a boy you had fathered but never seen? How much inane chitchat had to be spoken before anything important could be said? Did he even have the right to ask questions of this young man who had yet to remove his sunglasses?

James was surprised Kevin had come on his own, although grateful that he had. Having Paul there, too, might have been even more awkward. "How is Paul?"

"My father died a year ago."

James looked away, sadness rushing in. He closed his eyes. His throat tightened. He hadn't seen Paul in almost nineteen years, but he could see his face, hear his voice. "I'm sorry. Very sorry."

"Thanks." Kevin shoved his sunglasses on top of his head. His jaw twitched. "I'm not here looking for a father to replace him."

Kevin was angry. James understood that. His father was dead, and James lived. It wasn't fair. Life wasn't fair. "I wouldn't expect to take his place. He raised you."

"I heard you're a P.I."

Surprise zipped through him. "How'd you find that out?"

"From my mom. Last week she found the agreement between you and Dad. She checked you out."

Smart woman, not to let her son go blindly into a situation. But James wondered what she would've done if he hadn't passed muster. "I hope to meet her sometime."

One side of Kevin's mouth lifted. "My mom's kinda unpredictable."

"Okay." James didn't know what else to say. Did *unpredictable* mean crazy? Would she be a problem? "Does she know you're here?"

"No. And we're going to keep it that way."

"Why?"

"Because she wouldn't approve."

Which made no sense to James. "But you said she

checked me out, and obviously she gave you my name and address. That sounds like approval to me."

"She was keeping Dad's promise, that's all."

"I see. But you're here. Why?"

"Because there's something you can do for me."

"What's that?"

"Help me find my father's killer."

Stunned, James studied the boy, noting his fury and pain. "Killer?"

Kevin nodded once, sharply. "The cops say it was an accident. I know better."

A group of trick-or-treaters approached. James divided the remainder of his candy among them, tossing a handful into each bag.

"Cool!" a couple of them said before running off. "Thanks!"

James stood. "Let's go inside," he said to Kevin.

After a moment Kevin stood, too. James saw his own DNA in the boy, not like looking in a mirror, but as if Kevin had stepped out of James's high school yearbook. Did Kevin see it? Did it make him uncomfortable? James and Paul had shared some similarities, but not like this.

He turned off the porch light to discourage more trick-or-treaters, then watched Kevin look around his house, wondering what he thought of it. Sometimes the echoing quiet overwhelmed James.

"You live here alone?" Kevin asked, his hands shoved in his pockets again.

"Yes." He gestured toward the living room.

"Got any kids?"

Just you. "No."

"How come?"

"Until last year I worked as a bounty hunter. I wasn't home much. Didn't seem fair to a family to be gone so much."

He hesitated a few seconds. "My dad was gone a lot, too."

"What did he do?"

"Stuntman."

James sat in an overstuffed chair, deciding he would seem less intimidating sitting down. Kevin moved slowly around the room, stopping to look at an item, then moving on.

"Hollywood type?" James asked.

"Yeah."

"Seems like his death would've made news."

Kevin picked up a piece of yellow quartz that sat on the mantel and examined it. "It did."

"Maybe I was out of the country. Where'd you live?"

"In Southern California, in the Valley. Near Sylmar. We had a small ranch."

"With horses?"

"Yeah. Can't be an all-around stuntman if you can't ride." His tone of voice implied that James was being stupid for asking.

"I suppose not. You ride?"

"Of course."

Of course. "Your mom, too?"

Kevin faced him squarely. "Will you help me?"

So, no more chitchat. Kevin didn't care about James beyond what he could do for him, but it was enough for now. "Tell me what you know."

The boy drew himself up. Obviously, even a year later, he had trouble talking about the accident.

"Dad was riding his bike down the canyon road. It was raining. He and the bike went over the side."

"Why do you think it was intentional?"

"My dad was careful. Supercareful. He checked every stunt ten times. And he knew every inch of that road. No way that could've happened. No way."

"Even though it was raining?"

"He would've been supercautious."

The determination in his voice was convincing. "Yet the police think otherwise."

"The police didn't know my dad." He planted his feet and crossed his arms. "Look, if you don't want to help me, just say so."

"Had he been acting differently, Kevin? Do you have something concrete to go on?"

"Yes. Different. I don't know how to describe it. Just different."

"In what way?"

He closed his eyes for a few seconds. "Not there. I know that doesn't make sense. He was there, around, but he wasn't *there*. Like he was distracted all the time."

"Did you talk to him about it?"

"Sort of. I asked him if something was wrong, but he said no. He was just tired."

"You didn't believe him?"

Kevin shook his head. "I let it go, because I thought I would just give him some time. He told me everything. I figured he'd tell me this, too."

Not everything, apparently. Layered over the boy's obvious grief was belligerence, probably to hide how much he hurt. James's decision was easy. He would help Kevin—because if he didn't, Kevin would probably disappear from his life as quickly as he'd come into it, but also because James needed to help Kevin end his pain, or find a way to live with it, if he could. If Kevin would let him.

James also understood Kevin's urgency for justice.

"I'll investigate it," James told him.

"You don't sound like you believe me."

"I believe you knew your dad better than anyone, except your mom, probably. I just don't want you to get your hopes up."

"Are you good?"

"Yes."

Kevin stared at him. Wariness dulled his eyes, and he looked ready to flee at any moment. Finally he moved his shoulders, more an involuntary gesture of relief than an adolescent I-don't-care shrug. James figured he cared a whole lot.

"I'll need a little more information," James said, standing. "Let me get a pad of paper. Can I get you something to eat or drink while I'm up?"

"Not hungry."

The doorbell rang. James ignored it, assuming it was trick-or-treaters. He grabbed a pad from his office, convinced Kevin to sit down, then James wrote down more details—exactly where and when the accident occurred. Which police agencies were involved. More exact descriptions of Paul's out-of-character behavior.

"I can start with this," James said. "Give me a couple of days to do some preliminary digging. Do you want me to call you?"

Kevin swallowed hard then nodded.

James pretended not to see how much his help meant to Kevin. "What's your phone number and address?"

Kevin gave him a telephone number only. "It's my cell."

It was twice in a week that someone was afraid to give James personal information. An image of the Harley wrecker flashed in his mind. She'd had the same sort of wariness in her eyes as Kevin.

"I gotta go," Kevin said, pushing himself up. He hadn't taken off his jacket, and now he dropped his sunglasses back into place—before he headed out into the night.

James didn't want him to go, but he understood that if he wanted a relationship with this young man, he'd better take it slowly. He'd been handed a golden opportunity to get to know Kevin. He wouldn't squander it because he rushed it.

James extended his hand. Kevin clasped it. "Thanks," he mumbled, then he headed for the door, his strides long and quick. The door shut behind him with a rattle of glass. His footsteps down the stairs were heavy and fast, drifting out of earshot within seconds.

Silence crash landed louder than ever before in the big house James loved. He hadn't realized just how empty it was, not truly. It made him hunger to fill it up now. Right now.

He grabbed a beer and headed into his office. He would look up newspaper articles about Paul's death first. But when he pulled up a chair to the computer, he just sat there, thinking about Paul, about how they met, and what had happened between them to make James indebted to him.

He needed to tell someone. Not his mother, not yet. Not until the relationship settled. Quinn was in Los Angeles helping the other ARC owners on a big case. That left Cassie. He called her home number and got her answering machine. He hung up, debating whether to call her cell, which would be on, but he didn't want to interrupt her night with her fiancé. They weren't at home, so they must be out having fun somewhere.

The doorbell rang. As before, he ignored it. It rang again.

Fifteen seconds later, again. Irritated he headed to the front door. When he was a kid, an unlit porch light meant "do not disturb." He didn't have candy left to give out.

He yanked open the door, intending to give an etiquette lesson to the trick-or-treater. No costumed kid stood there, however, but the Harley wrecker, not decked out in a costume but in blue jeans and a red sweater.

"Am I interrupting something?" she asked, looking ready to flee, probably because he was scowling.

"No." He was surprised by the jolt of reaction that whipped through him. "No, please. Come in."

"Um. No, thank you. I'm sorry for dropping by so late, but I saw your light on. I just wanted to know about the estimate on the repairs. If I owe you more money."

Maybe it was because he was already high on adrenaline from meeting Kevin that his heart started beating louder. That was part of it, he supposed, but more likely it was because he found her appealing. He liked that she was a woman of her word, that she'd shown up when she said she would, proving that such people did exist. He also liked the wary look in her eyes, similar, in fact, to Kevin's expression, even the same shade of blue—

"Mr. Paladin?" she said, taking a step back, her expression even warier.

"Would you like to have dinner?" he asked. He needed to talk to someone about what had just happened. He had a feeling she would sympathize or cheer or give him good advice on how to handle the situation. Maybe she even had teenagers herself.

"With you?" she asked.

He smiled at the shock in her voice. "I can't really invite you to go out with anyone else, can I?"

"No, thank you," she said firmly. "Do I owe you more money?"

He was disappointed but not surprised at her turndown. "My mechanic hasn't given me an answer. If you'll leave your name and number this time, I'll give you a call when I know."

"I'll come back." She went down the stairs.

James watched her until she was out of sight, admiring the sway of her rear in her formfitting jeans. Although slender, she wasn't lacking curves in all the right places.

He wondered why he found her so intriguing, especially since she didn't flirt, and talked to him only as a person intent on doing business. In fact she'd looked at him at one point as if he'd had the plague. Physically she tempted him, but that wasn't all there was to it.

Deciding to ignore his disappointment, he fastened on his leather chaps, changed his shoes to boots, grabbed his jacket and helmet and headed out of the house. He needed company and he wanted a drink. He would find both—and do a little work at the same time.

Her nerves shot, Caryn sat in her car to unwind. About the time she would've driven away, she saw James come down the stairs, get on the motorcycle parked out front— his loaner, she guessed—and take off.

She followed him. She wasn't even sure why, except that she was leaving at the same time and—

No. That wasn't the truth. The truth was that she was fascinated by him. He'd obviously done well for himself, if his house was any indicator. He looked really good dressed in jeans and a T-shirt, too. Like a normal person— except for the scruffy beard. Not like a biker, a risk taker, an adventurer. Like Paul.

Caryn wished she could show James a picture of Kevin, to talk about her wonderful son, to thank the man for his generosity in making Kevin's life possible. To ask why he'd done it. But she couldn't. Kevin had to make the overture, and he didn't seem inclined to do so yet.

She'd been tempted—too tempted—to go to dinner with James. She was already withholding information from him—for good reason—but anything more could be interpreted as lies. If Kevin ever contacted him, and she and James met officially, it could be disastrous with lies between them. So far everything she'd done was forgivable, under the circumstances.

She let a car get between hers and his motorcycle, hoping he hadn't spotted her. She wanted to know where he was headed after she'd turned him down.

The adventure of following him revved her up. She smiled at the excitement clamoring inside her. It was the last thing she needed, really, this adrenaline rush, this risky scenario. She'd just gotten her life together after Paul's death. She didn't need this kind of complication.

If only James didn't push so many of her hot buttons—like the fantasy of finally meeting him, and the deep-down wish for Kevin to have a father again, a male influence, an anchor.

And then there was that other hot button—a year without intimacy. Her body had come back to life with a vengeance, just by being near him.

She realized he was driving, not in circles exactly, but as if trying to lose her. After a few more turns and cutbacks he pulled up in front of a loud and seedy bar where the street was full of parked motorcycles, some mean-looking ones.

She realized she was lost. Didn't have a clue where she

was or how to get home from there. Worst of all, he'd spotted her. It was ridiculous of her to even try driving past him when he stared right into her car.

She slowed to a stop. He came up alongside her driver's window, pulled off his helmet.

"Change your mind?" he asked.

"About what?"

"Having dinner with me."

"No."

"Why were you following me?"

"I don't know."

His brows lifted.

"Okay. Frankly, I was curious. Beyond that, I don't have a clue. Honestly. I saw you pull out, and I just…followed. And now I'm lost because you were trying to lose me, and I was focused on staying with you instead of on where I was."

"If I'd wanted to lose you, I would have," he said blandly.

Of course. She should've known that. "You were playing a game with me?"

"I was seeing if you were following me. You were." He leaned an arm against the top of her car. "The invitation holds, Mysterious."

She glanced at the bar as another bike pulled up. A beefy man helped a woman climb off it. Both of them had tattoos down their arms and around their necks.

"Not here," he said with a quick, contagious grin.

"I'll bet that smile works, most of the time," she said, relaxing. He hadn't done anything to intimidate her, even if she'd felt intimidated at times. But that was her problem, not his.

"You intrigue me," he said.

She did? She was so straightforward, usually, and so…unintriguing. Was it because she was keeping herself mysterious, and therefore, hard to get? Instead of telling him he was ridiculous, that she was the least intriguing person on earth, she smiled. "Then I should keep doing what I'm doing," she said leisurely.

"Ah. It's the chase that excites you."

She started to flirt back, then realized she had no right to. What was she thinking? She gathered up her long-denied, flattered libido and adjusted her body language and tone of voice. "How do I get back to Market?"

He barely skipped a beat before giving her directions, then he took a step back. His smile disappeared.

"I'll see you in a couple of days," she said.

He nodded.

She felt awful as she pulled away, like a big tease, like a teenager without any life skills. She'd responded to him without thinking it through. She was sinking deeper into a situation she should be avoiding at all costs.

And she was afraid she wasn't going to be able to stop.

Four

James's usual way of doing business was to put together a binder containing copies of his research and phone log to give to the client as the investigation progressed. For purely selfish reasons, he did none of it for Kevin, deciding that the boy might just take the materials and run. Instead he would have to come in and stay awhile to hear the results of James's initial inquiry. If nothing else, it would give them some time together. Maybe it wouldn't only be about business.

It was Tuesday afternoon, three days since Kevin had appeared in his life. James had lived in a kind of fog, focusing enough to work, but easily distracted, not only because of Kevin but also Mysterious.

He wasn't sure what to think of her. She'd followed him, flirted with him, then shut him down. Not a woman who knew her own mind at all. Unpredictable…

Which is what Kevin had called his mother, too. Apparently it was the watchword for the modern woman. But he preferred unpredictable to the expected, anyway.

James had called Kevin's cell phone a while ago, had caught him leaving his last class of the day. He was on his way.

Deciding that the way to a teenage boy's heart was through his stomach, James set bowls of salsa and chips on the kitchen counter, deciding the kitchen would be a less intimidating place to talk than in the living room.

He wandered to the front window to watch for Kevin's arrival. Anxiety ate away at him. Nothing in his experience had prepared him for this. No matter what he did or said, Kevin could perceive him as trying too hard or not hard enough, or whatever else was within the realm of possibility in a teenager's mind.

He wondered why Kevin didn't want his mother to know they'd met, but he was grateful she'd considered Paul's promise sacred. Realistically, however, how long did Kevin think he could keep it from his mother?

Kevin came into sight, hands shoved in his pockets, sunglasses in place, a Dodgers cap on his head. Where had he parked? There were empty spots in front of the house, but he was on foot. The bigger question, though—should James open the door before Kevin reached it or wait for him to knock? He hated that he didn't know how to behave with Kevin. Would Kevin want to know how anxious James was to see him—or would he think James's expectations were too high?

He decided to let the boy ring the bell, then opened the door almost instantly. "How's it going?" James asked, heading toward the kitchen, letting Kevin follow.

"Okay."

"I figured you might be hungry." He pointed toward the snacks. "What do you drink?"

"Orange juice."

Hiding a smile, James opened the refrigerator and grabbed the juice, shutting the door on six different brands of soda he'd bought, hoping that one was Kevin's favorite. He poured a tall glass, was pleased that Kevin was already eating the chips and salsa, which seemed an odd combination with orange juice.

"You going to college full-time?" James asked.

"Eighteen units."

"What's your major?"

"Criminal justice." His gaze strayed to the folder James had left on the counter. "You find out anything?"

Criminal justice. Same as Paul and me. James didn't sit in the chair next to Kevin, but left an empty seat between them. "I found out a lot, but I doubt it's anything you don't already know."

The doorbell rang. James excused himself. "I'm expecting a package," he said. "I'll be right back."

It was a package, all right, but not the one he expected. This one was about five feet seven, reed slender and dressed in her waitress garb of white blouse and black skirt. "Mysterious," he said as coolly as he could. She'd irritated him the other night with her flirtation game, or whatever it was, but he couldn't seem to convince his tap-dancing hormones that he should stay detached.

"Hi. I happened to be in the neighborhood." She smiled nervously.

"I've got company. Could you come back in a while?"

Impatience flickered in her eyes. "How much time do

you need to give me an answer? Yes, I owe you more money, and how much—or, no, I don't."

He could give her an answer. He didn't want to. Not yet. Obviously there was something between them. He needed to know why she was resisting exploring their attraction. "I—"

"You *followed* me?"

Kevin stormed up beside James, but the shouted words were directed to the Harley wrecker.

"Kevin!" Her eyes went from Kevin to James and back again. "I didn't. I didn't know you were—"

"I told you, Mom! I *told* you. I have to find my father's killer."

Mom? Well, everything made sense to James now. Or maybe not everything, but a lot. One thing was crystal clear, however. Kevin's accusation of his mother following him was way off base. James could see her genuine shock that Kevin was there.

"I'm eighteen," Kevin said. "You can't tell me what to do anymore."

"I did not follow you." Her voice was steady, her posture stiff, her color high, almost matching her red lipstick.

He turned on James, glaring. "So you were part of this? You called *her*, too? Thanks for nothing."

James grabbed his arm as he started to leave. "Not so fast. I don't know for sure what's going on, but I can guess. Both of you come in and we'll talk this out."

Kevin tried to jerk his arm free. "Let go of me."

"Son—"

"I'm not your son."

It was only a slip of the tongue, brought about perhaps by a little wishful thinking. "I apologize, Kevin. But listen for a second. Your mother and I met the other day, but I had no idea who she was. She's here because she backed into my bike, and she's paying for the damages, not because we were conspiring together over you." He fired a look at Caryn. "Or maybe she'll contact her insurance company instead, now."

Caryn couldn't have cared less about the bike repairs. Seeing the hurt and anger in Kevin's eyes brought back the other times in the past year when she'd had to stop him from going off on his own to investigate Paul's death. She'd thought he'd finally accepted the police findings that his father died in an accident, not by sabotage, not with intent to kill him.

Obviously Kevin hadn't. She needed to stop him, needed for him to believe the police before something happened to him, too.

"I'm outta here," he said, rushing off, leaving a red haze of anger in the air behind him.

"Kevin—"

"I'm going home. That's all."

"Come in," James said to Caryn, unsmiling, his voice steady.

His house was like something out of *Architectural Digest*. Large and airy rooms decorated in a classic style, with hardwood floors, large area rugs, and comfortable but stylish furnishings. Rich fabrics invited touch; gleaming wood drew the eye. The interior suited the architecture of the house, if not the man, at least what little she knew of him.

She sat on a suede-covered sofa. He took a seat in a chair nearby and leaned forward, his arms resting on his thighs.

"So," he said.

She waited for the punch line.

"A few things you forgot to mention, Mysterious?"

"If I hadn't hit your fender, you wouldn't have known I existed," she said. Hardly a winning argument.

"But you did hit my fender. Why didn't you just tell me who you were?"

Fight fire with fire, she decided. She needed to work through her shock and anger first that Kevin had been there. "Why did you give Paul a wrong address?"

He frowned. "Excuse me?"

"In the letter you sent to Paul with your new address, you gave him the number of a house across the street. Why?"

"I rented there while my house was being renovated. I moved in here a couple of months ago. I...forgot to send another note. I would've remembered soon, though, I promise you that. And my phone number was the same as I wrote. Now, again, why didn't you just tell me who you were?"

"I wanted to, but the decision to have contact with you was Kevin's to make. I went home and reported to him everything I knew, because it was the right thing to do. He *told* me he didn't want to meet you."

He sat back. Was that disappointment in his eyes? "But he did come to meet me."

"He didn't tell me he had. Probably because he knew I wouldn't have approved—not for the reason I figure he decided to see you, anyway."

"To get my help in finding Paul's killer."

She nodded. She wasn't sure how much to tell him about her own suspicions.

"Do you think he was murdered, Caryn?"

"It has been ruled an accident."

"That wasn't my question."

She gave him as much truth as she thought necessary. "Paul was a gambler."

"And that ties in to his death how?"

"I don't know." It was speculation on her part, which she didn't want to share with him. He would probably come up with the same answers as the police about Paul's death. If so, it should end Kevin's interest forever, and he would be safe.

"I think you do know." James leaned forward again. His eyes searched hers. "Was Paul in debt?"

"Yes. But that debt is paid now."

"How?"

"I paid it."

He studied her in silence. She didn't break eye contact.

"Did you have anything left?" he asked.

"Enough."

"Enough for what?"

She pushed herself off the couch then didn't know what to do, so she walked to the fireplace and took a closer look at the painting hanging there, a scene out of Greece, she thought, with red-tile roofs, white buildings and cypress trees. She wished she were there. "Enough to get Kevin through college. Enough to buy a duplex here."

"But nothing for your future."

"Both of those items qualify as *future* to me."

"I mean something toward your own retirement." He stood then, too, and came up beside her.

She tried to look nonchalant, but his proximity tempted her in ways she shouldn't be tempted. Not with him, of all people. "I've got a long ways until retirement."

"You work as a waitress?"

"Yeah, so? It's a decent profession. I waited tables a lot when I was young."

"I was not insulting you, Caryn. I'm curious about your life, especially life with Paul."

"We boarded horses. It was something we both—all three of us—did. It was a lot of work."

"Why did you move to San Francisco?"

"It's home for me." And she needed to get away from the Valley and all its memories—and future worries.

"You have family here?"

She was getting impatient with his questions, even as she understood why he had them. "Not anymore, but Kevin decided to go to college here and I decided to come home. It's worked out fine." She crossed her arms.

"You don't like that he got in touch with me," James said.

"No."

"Why not?"

Because you will intrigue him. You take risks, like his father did. He will be enthralled. And I will be relegated to the background.

"Never mind," James said. He laid a hand on her shoulder. "I think I know. I'm not going to take him away from you. I couldn't if I tried."

His touch was electric. She tried to ignore the feeling and the unbidden thought that she hadn't been touched by a man in nearly a year, 361 days to be precise. Every neuron snapped to attention and saluted. Every hormone wanted to break ranks and mutiny.

She shoved that thought to the back of her mind. "Look," she said as calmly as possible. "I'll hire you to do a full investigation. Just keep Kevin out of it."

"I can't do that."

She turned away from him, hurt and angry. How could she protect her son? How much would she have to reveal to James to get him to back off or at least investigate on his own?

"Kevin needs to be involved," he said. "He loved his father. It's a point of honor for him. If he doesn't get an answer that satisfies him, he'll never rest. I know this because I would feel the same in his position. He needs to be part of the process. I'll protect him. He'll be safe."

How can you guarantee that? she wanted to scream, feeling handcuffed. If she didn't give in, she stood to alienate her son, and she was afraid of that. She'd already lost too much in the past year, including whatever innocence about the world she'd had. And her relationship with Kevin had become stormy, as well, worse since he'd turned eighteen last month.

"I want to be involved, too," she said, turning to face James, keeping her expression neutral.

He was silent for several long seconds. "All right. But let's tell Kevin it was my idea. I think he'll take it better if I make it part of the deal."

"I can live with that."

One side of his mouth lifted in an appealing half smile.

How was she going to work with him with this attraction clawing at her? He had a way of focusing on her, eye to eye, his attention fully engaged, that she liked. She hadn't been listened to so well in…a very long time. Then again, she'd learned why Paul had stopped looking her in the eye—guilt.

"I'll give him a call right now," James said, then punched in a number on his cell phone.

The doorbell rang. His phone to his ear, he opened the door then signed for a package. He tossed it on a chair then returned to the living room. "Kevin," he said into the phone, "this is James. I want to continue the investigation. When you get this message, call me. Better yet, come on back and talk."

He snapped the phone shut. "Voice mail."

"So, now what?" Caryn asked.

"We wait. Are you hungry?"

She was surprised that she was. Her stomach had been tied in knots until a minute ago. "I could eat something."

"I've got stuff to make sandwiches. Let's eat while we wait for your son."

She followed him to the back of the house into a beautiful kitchen with white cabinets, stainless steel appliances and granite countertops. The mix of old and new worked, for the house *and* the man, this time, now that she knew he wasn't part of a biker gang.

He pulled a deli tray from the refrigerator, grabbed a bag of sourdough sandwich rolls and set them on the counter. She had questions for him, questions she'd prefer to ask without Kevin there.

She was also enjoying sitting at his kitchen counter and watching him move around the kitchen. The distraction prevented her from firing the first salvo.

"What can you tell me about Paul's death that isn't in the police report?" he asked.

"What makes you think there's more?"

He met her gaze and held it, his eyes boring into hers, his expression serious, probably a skill from his bounty hunter days.

"Okay," she said. "There's more."

She should've known he wouldn't leave things alone.

Five

James had no doubt there was "more." His suspicions weren't aroused by anything in the police report but by Caryn's body language. He knew when someone wasn't telling the truth, and her face was more open than most. He wanted to keep his distance, now that he knew who she was. But the attraction wasn't fading, and in fact was only being added to as he learned more about her—which was not a good sign.

"Tell me about the gambling," he said, the food going untouched.

"There are things I don't want Kevin to know."

"You call the shots."

She studied him for several long seconds before saying okay. "I can only tell you what I've learned since he died. I wasn't aware of it before, except that I often wondered why we weren't doing better financially than we were."

Her hands were folded in her lap. Her expression seemed neutral, but hurt dulled her eyes. Too many burdens, he decided. Too much to handle alone, as she undoubtedly had. Shame like that wasn't something people confided in others, especially a woman like Caryn, who wore her independence openly.

"Some men came to the house right after the funeral. They had notes, IOUs."

"Signed by Paul?"

"Yes."

"For how much?"

"Eight hundred thousand."

Fury snaked through James, although he wasn't sure whether it was directed at the men or Paul. "You believed them?"

"Not at first. You hear about all sorts of scams that people try to pull on the family after someone dies, so I ordered them off my property. I had my phone in my hand, and I started to call the police. They told me if I did, that…" She closed her eyes and swallowed.

"That they would harm Kevin?"

She nodded. "Um, they told me to check out my bank statements and his pay statements, and all the other financial paperwork that Paul had always taken care of. They gave me a week. Then they came back. Well, that's not true. Someone was always hanging around the property, making sure I didn't run away, I guess."

He could only imagine her fear. She should've involved the police, but he couldn't tell her that, not now that it was too late to do anything differently. "You found out they were right?" he asked.

"I couldn't verify the exact amount, but there should've

been a lot more money invested. And then there were the intangibles—I didn't know how much he'd won and lost, how much cash he would bet after a big win—or whatever he did. But we should've had a lot more in the bank, that much I know." She tucked her hair behind her ears. "I can't believe I was so stupid. He'd always said he was handling it, and yet we never seemed to have enough. We didn't even have horses of our own. We boarded other people's."

"Why didn't you question him if that was something that bothered you?"

"What can I say? It would be like complaining that he wasn't taking care of us. I loved him. I trusted him. I knew he took risks—he always had. It just never crossed my mind that he was taking financial risks."

A hard lesson learned for her. She would never trust in the same way again, he thought.

"How did you come up with the payoff, Caryn?"

"Insurance."

"They waited that long for payment?"

"Oh, sure. Mr. Nice Guys. They just demanded their pound of flesh with it."

James's world exploded red. *"What?"*

"Not that. Not me," she said quickly, a hand outstretched. "I meant interest. Fortunately, because of the nature of his business, being a stuntman, he was well insured, and he'd never missed a payment."

James drew a slow breath, settling himself. "Then you sold your ranch and moved here."

"I wanted to come home. I wanted to feel the fog and climb the hills and smell the ocean again. I wanted hustle and bustle."

"Were you isolated on the ranch?"

She jumped as the doorbell rang. He put a hand on her shoulder until she relaxed. He could kill Paul for what he'd put her through. Jolted at his thoughts, he pulled back mentally. Too close, too fast.

"Let's hope it's Kevin," he said, heading out of the kitchen.

"You won't tell him about, you know, Paul and—"

"I won't." He felt as protective as she did, although he wasn't sure that withholding the truth from Kevin was the best course of action. If he found out sometime about what his father had done…

"You said you would continue the investigation," Kevin said, accusation in his voice when James opened the door. "But my mom's car is still here."

"I want her involved."

"I don't—"

"She has every right to be a part of this," James said, interrupting. He couldn't threaten to back out, because he was afraid Kevin would do what he'd planned—investigate on his own.

"Fine," the boy said after several long seconds had passed.

"Are you hungry? We'll figure out what we're going to do while we eat." He wanted to put an arm around Kevin's shoulders as they walked. He knew he couldn't call himself a father, except in the loosest sense of the word, but he felt protective of Kevin already, and paternal. Maybe because he'd known all these years that he had a child out there somewhere, he'd harbored feelings that only needed physical contact to come to life. He sensed that beneath Kevin's belligerence was a deep-down grief that James wouldn't be able to erase, but maybe he could alleviate it some by finding the truth for him.

And now that James knew about Paul's gambling and the vultures who'd descended at word of his death, he realized Kevin might very well be right—that Paul was murdered.

James watched Caryn give Kevin a hug. After a few seconds, Kevin returned it briefly, then he took a seat at the opposite end of the counter, leaving two empty seats between mother and son—which meant James would have to sit next to either Caryn or Kevin.

He walked around the counter instead and set the deli platter between them to let them make their own sandwiches. He stayed where he was, standing, able to observe them more easily.

"This doesn't have to be awkward," James said, looking back and forth between them. "It's an unusual situation, I'll grant you that, but there isn't any reason why we can't be comfortable with each other."

"It's just…weird," Kevin said.

"I agree, but for now why don't we just focus on what brought you here in the first place."

"My father's murder."

"His death, anyway," James said. He watched Kevin build a huge sandwich and felt a certain satisfaction in seeing him relax enough to eat. "Was the wreckage of his motorcycle retained by the police?" he asked Caryn.

"Yes."

"I'll see if it's stored anywhere. If so, I can have it shipped up to my mechanic and let him take a look."

As they ate, they looked at the report James had put together. None of it was new to Kevin.

"What do you think we can find out that's different?" he asked James. "Who do we talk to?"

James resisted looking at Caryn. He knew she was

right—for now—that Kevin not be apprised of his father's gambling connections. Going headstrong into that criminal quicksand could be lethal. But he didn't have another realistic clue for Kevin to follow.

"Tell me why you think he was murdered," he said.

"Gut instinct. He must've known something. Or seen something. There's always something going on in Hollywood."

"That's pretty vague."

"Look. I know my father. He knew that road! Someone did something."

"Kevin's right about him knowing the road," Caryn agreed, picking up the plates and walking around the counter. She turned on the faucet. "But it had been raining…"

Kevin turned on her. "Like that had never happened before? Come on, Mom. Get real."

James interrupted. "Okay, first things first. I'll try to track down the wreckage. Caryn, have you gone through all his paperwork, anything that might lead to a clue? Someone needs to go through all that very thoroughly. Analyze it." He hoped she got his hidden message that he wanted busywork for Kevin.

"I haven't sorted everything," she said.

"I'll go through it," Kevin volunteered. "Okay, Mom?"

"Sure."

Finally showing some enthusiasm, he tossed his napkin on the counter and sprang out of the chair.

"Right this second?" Caryn asked.

"Yeah. I'll meet you at home. Bye."

"Hang on," James said.

Kevin stood still. He crossed his arms.

"I need something in return."

James felt Caryn's gaze. He should've talked it over with her first, but there hadn't been any opportunity. "My father died last year, too," James said. Kevin's expression didn't change. "My mother has been lonely and pretty depressed, as I'm sure you can imagine. Knowing about you, meeting you, would be good for her."

"No way I—"

"It's the only thing I'll ask of you."

Silence hung in the air. James didn't take his eyes off Kevin. Caryn said nothing. Would she intervene if Kevin said no?

"Okay," he said finally, then he left.

The front door shut hard. Caryn turned to James. "I'm sure he meant to say thank you for dinner and for helping him—us—find out the truth."

"Remains to be seen. If it was organized crime Paul was involved in, we probably won't get answers, not without endangering one or all of us."

"I don't want that."

"I know."

Drying her hands on a dish towel, she leaned against the counter. "I'm sorry for misleading you last week."

"I understand why you did it." *But what are we going to do about the attraction that was so obvious? You followed me, flirted with me.* "I'm sorry I didn't talk to you first about my mother."

"If someone had offered me that kind of distraction during the worst of my mourning, I would've been grateful."

"Will you give me your phone number now?" he asked, pushing a notepad in her direction.

She smiled, then wrote down the information.

"When do you work?" he asked.

"Monday through Friday from 6:00 a.m. to 3:00 p.m."

"Where?"

She fished a set of keys from her pocket. "At the GGC."

The GGC, or Golden Gate Club, was a private golf and tennis club almost as old as the Golden Gate Bridge. The shift she worked wouldn't be as lucrative as evenings and weekends. She would probably have to be there for a while to garner those premium shifts.

She jingled her keys. "Kevin has a crush on one of my coworkers, Venus."

He grinned. "Venus? Does she look like a goddess?"

"Pretty much, yeah." Her eyes finally took on some sparkle. "She's twenty-three, blond, bubbly and with a body straight out of every teenage boy's dream."

"When can I meet her?"

She smiled. He might have, too, except it struck him that Cassie would've reminded him that it wasn't unusual for him to date women that age.

"Maybe you'll talk to him about it, give him some advice," Caryn said.

"Like, wear a condom?"

She gave him that cool look he'd liked so much the other day, and he laughed, then lightly touched her arm.

"He's eighteen, Mysterious. Eighteen-year-old boys like the kind of woman you've described. They like them a lot. What kind of interaction do they have?"

"Interaction?"

"Do they talk? Or flirt? Does she treat him like a kid brother? Does she cozy up to him?"

"She doesn't discourage him."

"When do they see each other?"

"She's new to waiting tables and has no family in San

Francisco. I kind of took her under my wing. She's around, off and on."

"Does Kevin have a job?"

"He's been putting in applications here and there but nothing so far."

"Want me to see what I can do?"

Her brows lifted. "That would be great."

"What's he looking for?"

"He's very good in math, not so good with the written word, is fascinated by guns and is a pretty good athlete."

"So, he can deliver pizzas?"

She laughed, a no-cares sound that pleased him. It had taken a long string of conversation to get her to relax to that point.

"Is this as weird for you as it is for me?" he asked as they walked to the front door.

"Weirder." She sounded relieved to voice it out loud.

"It changes what we got started last week, doesn't it?"

She fixed her gaze on him. "What we got started?"

"The flirtation," he said, testing the waters. He needed to know where he stood, how to proceed with a relationship that was bizarre, yet oddly right. "Or was that a game to throw me off track?"

"You want the truth?"

"Absolutely."

"I couldn't help myself." She blew out a breath. "I know that complicates things."

He shoved his hands in his pockets. "I guess we'll just take it a day at a time."

She nodded. He appreciated that she didn't discount the attraction, especially since it sat there between them like a curious creature out of a vivid dream.

"Why'd you do it?" she asked.

"Do what?"

"Agree to the artificial insemination."

The reason flashed like lightning in James's mind, but he doused it. "That's a story for another day, I think. Kevin is waiting for you."

"Now you have me curious, James."

"My friends call me Jamey. You're welcome to, if you want."

"You're ducking the issue."

"I'd rather tell you when we have more time." He opened the front door for her. "How much busywork are you giving Kevin by having him go through Paul's papers?"

"Depends how fast he works. There's actually quite a bit. Maybe I can get him to organize and file it, which is something I haven't gotten around to doing."

"Are you sure he won't find anything that would link Paul to the gambling? Something Kevin might go off on his own about, thinking he was taking care of business?"

She frowned. "No, I'm not sure. But I will emphasize to him that he needs to share whatever he finds."

"Even though *we* won't be?"

"I know it's not fair, but his safety is more important."

"I agree. But I also think we can tell him the truth and still keep him safe."

"Maybe. We'll talk about it." She put out her hand. "Thank you."

He clasped her hand with both of his. "My pleasure."

"You took my deceit better than I would've expected."

"I understand your motivation." He liked the feel of her hand in his, the delicate bones and not-too-soft skin. Her nails, he'd noted before, were short and clean, unpolished.

Neither of them let go. She met his gaze.

"You can trust me, Caryn."

"I do. You can trust me, as well."

"I know that."

She seemed about to say something else, then pulled her hand free. "We'll be in touch?"

"Yeah."

"Okay. Bye."

He didn't watch her walk down the stairs, thinking it might make her uncomfortable. Instead he shut the door and went to the living room window, staying far enough back that she couldn't see him. When she got to her car she looked up and stared at the house for several long seconds. Something hot and vital detonated inside him. Dangerous. She was dangerous. No one had upset his equilibrium as she had, not with a look, a small touch…and a huge connection, he added, acknowledging the most important issue—Kevin.

James should keep his distance from Caryn, deal mostly with Kevin, if he could, and build that relationship without his mother being a part of the day-to-day contact. It would be too strange for them to take this relationship to a place of impossibility. How could they have more than the sharing of a child?

They couldn't. James wanted marriage *and* children. How could that include Caryn? And what about Kevin?

Overnight, James's life had changed irrevocably. There was no vague wife-and-children dream now, but a reality far different. Real people. Real dilemmas. The potential for hurt.

He would make no quick decisions.

Six

The next morning at the GGC, the breakfast crowd had dwindled to a few lingerers. In an hour the lunch patrons would start trickling in. Caryn came up beside Venus in the dining room and said quietly, "Table six is wondering where their juice is."

"Oh, shoot. Mind like a sieve," she said, rolling her eyes, grinning, then strolling toward the juice station.

Caryn bit off a sigh. Even after a month of training, Venus made beginner mistakes. Problem was, the mostly male customers couldn't care less. She would rectify the situation, bat her long-lashed hazel eyes, apologize sweetly and walk away, her hips swaying hypnotically, guaranteeing herself a full tip, if not higher than average—helped along perhaps, by the low-cut blouse that showed off the assets Kevin usually focused on when she was around. She packed a punch, Venus Johnson.

But it was impossible to dislike or resent her. Genuine, sweet, and sincerely intent on learning her job, she was unfortunately also without the skill to do it well. Yet no one on staff breathed a word about her being let go for incompetence, not even the manager, Rafael, who groused about everyone's work, even when they were doing a good job.

Caryn wondered if Venus would go through life forever having allowances made for her. At least she followed the rules of no fraternizing with the club members. Too bad those rules didn't apply to children of employees, Caryn thought. She was afraid Kevin would get his heart broken if Venus didn't stop being so attentive to him. He'd been in college for two months without showing an interest in a particular girl, even though he'd never had trouble finding dates. She'd fielded calls from giggling girls since he was in fifth grade.

"Mom."

Startled, Caryn turned around to find Kevin behind her. She looked around for the manager. "What are you doing here? You know I can't have visitors."

"Chill. Rafael said it was okay."

"You're kidding."

"Nope. He said you could take fifteen minutes." Kevin wasn't looking at her as he spoke but at Venus, who spotted him from across the dining room and waved. She headed to the beverage station, smiling, her blond curls bouncing.

Caryn noted the faint flush on Kevin's cheeks as Venus gave him a quick hug. Since Caryn was dealing with an infatuation of her own, she sympathized with Kevin as he struggled to find words.

"Did you come to see me?" Venus asked.

"No, well, I, um, came for…"

"Me," Caryn said. "And I've only got fifteen minutes. Can you watch table eleven for me, please? I think they're good for a little while, but if they want their check, let me know. We'll be in the break room."

"Sure. I was hoping I could stop by after work," Venus said, a hopeful lilt to her voice. "Maybe I'll see you then, Kevin?"

"I'm not sure. Got some stuff goin' on."

Kevin usually changed plans to be around whenever he knew Venus planned to stop by. Maybe his interest in her was waning? A silver lining to this investigation?

"Let's go," she said to her son, guiding him away. They reached the break room, a meager space not designed for comfort but for grabbing a quick bite to eat, putting your dog-tired feet up for a couple of minutes then returning to the floor refreshed, if such a thing were possible. "What's up?" she asked as they sat on the vinyl sofa. "Why aren't you in class?"

Kevin frowned. "It's Wednesday."

Oh. Right. He didn't go to school until 2:00 p.m. on Wednesday. Considering he'd been up most of the night going through the boxes of Paul's paperwork, she would've expected him to still be sleeping.

"Mr.… *He* called," he said.

Caryn didn't know whether the twinge in her midsection came from thoughts of James and how he'd touched her a couple of times yesterday—or if she was jealous that James had contacted Kevin and not her.

"What'd he say?"

"He wants me to meet his mother today."

"Today?"

"Fast, huh? Mom, what do I say to her?"

"I think you can count on James to guide the conversation. He will have told his mother everything in advance, I'm sure, not just drop in on her with you as a surprise."

"I know, but it's…weird. This whole thing is weird."

Tell me about it. Caryn wasn't sure how she felt about Kevin meeting the woman. What if their extraordinary relationship withered after they'd taken the investigation into Paul's death as far as they could? Was it fair to any of them to foster a connection with a grandparent, a loose term in this instance, when they didn't know how everything would turn out?

On the other hand, Caryn understood the woman's loneliness and depression after her husband's death. If Caryn hadn't had Kevin, she might have stayed in bed many, many days.

"James is doing us a favor," she said to her son. "It seemed really important to him. You, of all people, understand how hard her life must've been this past year."

"I know, Mom. I do. But, like, what do I say?"

"You make small talk. You answer questions. You ask her some questions, too. No one expects you to like each other instantly. It's going to seem awkward to her, too."

"Would you come? Please?"

She wanted to say yes, especially since he asked, and she was, in fact, a little miffed that James hadn't asked her. But the fact was she hadn't been invited, period. "If he'd wanted me there, he would've asked me. When are you meeting him?"

"At noon. At least, I can't stay long, with class at two o'clock." He shoved himself up, frustration evident in every taut muscle. "What if she asks me about Dad? I mean, her son is— You know. God, Mom. I can't even tell anyone about this."

"I know the feeling." She went to stand beside him and rubbed his back. "I'm sure it'll get easier with time."

"You and Dad couldn't just have adopted like a normal couple?" He grinned finally, silently acknowledging that he knew he wouldn't have been there without James's contribution.

She smiled. "I'll try to call you on your cell before your two o'clock class starts."

"Okay. I feel like I'm going up in front of a firing squad."

"I think I've got a bandanna somewhere if you want a blindfold."

He smiled.

She hugged him. "I'm proud of you, Kevin. Dad would be proud of you."

"Thanks."

"Sorry." Venus had opened the door. "Didn't mean to intrude. But your table is ready for their check."

"I'll be right there," Caryn said.

"If you give me the book I'll take care of it."

"No, it's all right."

With a curious look between Kevin and Caryn, Venus backed out of the room.

"Are you going to let her go home with you?" Kevin asked.

"I think so. It'll help me pass the time until you get out of school." And she could count on him coming straight home, knowing that Venus would be there.

She cut her break short and carried the bill wallet to table eleven. The next time she looked at her watch it was noon. A new chapter in Kevin's life was just beginning.

* * *

James had arrived at his mother's house at eleven-thirty, recited the history of Paul and Caryn and Kevin, then went outside to await Kevin's arrival. His mother had reacted pretty much as he'd expected—with reserved curiosity. Now all he could do was hope that Kevin didn't make things difficult. On the phone earlier Kevin had obviously wished himself to the moon instead of meeting James's mother.

It didn't matter to James if Kevin acknowledged him as a father, but he hoped in time his mother would be acknowledged as grandmother. She needed something to look forward to.

"Hey."

James turned, surprised. "Where'd you park?" he asked Kevin, who had his hands stuck in his pockets, a pose James was beginning to think he would always associate with him.

"Up the street. I like to get the lay of the land first."

"You'd make a good P.I.—or a cop."

"Yeah?"

Shoot. Caryn would kill him for making such a remark. She'd be about as pleased as his own mother when he announced his plan to become a bounty hunter. "Figure of speech," James said.

Kevin's mouth lifted in a half smile. "I won't tell Mom you said so."

"Thanks." He resisted the urge to put an arm around the boy's shoulders. "Ready to meet my mom?"

"Guess so."

James recognized Kevin's apprehension. "Just be yourself." They started up the stairs. "How's your mom?"

"Good. I stopped by and saw her at work. Told her I was coming here."

James had debated whether to invite her, but decided against it. Too many people might complicate a situation that should be as simple and nonthreatening as possible. But he also had no doubt his mother would pick up on the attraction between him and Caryn. No doubt at all. His mom would've made a good P.I. herself.

"Was she okay with it?" James asked.

"Guess so. She's pretty cool."

"But unpredictable, you said."

"Yeah. But that's what makes her cool. Sometimes."

"He's here," James called out after they'd stepped through the front door.

"She's baking cookies," Kevin said after sniffing the air. "Chocolate chip."

"Yeah?" After a second James nodded. He wondered how she could've made the dough so quickly. They wouldn't be from a store-bought cookie dough, that much he knew. She was the from-scratch queen. "Good nose."

She rounded the corner, wearing a bright pink apron over her purple jogging suit. Her ash-blond hair might have come from a bottle but the short style wasn't too matronly for her sixty-three years, nor too youthful. She wore classic but trendy clothes that suited her petite frame.

"You look just like Jamey did at—" She put both hands to her mouth. Her eyes took on some sheen. "Kevin," she said. "I'm so glad to meet you. I'm Emmaline."

A long moment of silence passed, then he grinned. "You made cookies."

"Come in the kitchen. They'll be done in two minutes." James started to follow.

"We'll be all right without you," Emmaline said over her shoulder. "You can get back to work."

Dismissed by his own mother, who would undoubtedly get to know all kinds of things about Kevin that he didn't know yet, maybe would never know. He refused to admit he was jealous. Kevin had smiled at his mother, a full, all-out grin, not holding back anything, not the nervous smile he'd given James a couple of times.

He hadn't expected this to be easy. Walls of resistance were hard to break down, after all. He knew he had to earn Kevin's respect and friendship, yet James's mother—

No. It was exactly what he wanted for her. Why shouldn't one part of this situation be easy? His mother and Kevin deserved that much.

James climbed into his car, pulled out his cell phone and dialed.

"Cassie Miranda."

"Hey, it's Jamey. Had lunch yet?"

"No, why?"

"Want to meet me at the GGC?"

Cassie whistled low. "You joined that fancy place?"

"No. But I have connections. I did a job for the board president a while back. I think he'll arrange admittance for me. I hear they do a killer filet mignon." He could almost hear her drooling.

"You buying?"

"I invited, didn't I? Can you leave now?"

"Sure. See you in fifteen."

James's next call was to the board president. So it was a bit of a subterfuge, taking Cassie along as if she were his lunch date, but he needed to tell Caryn about Kevin and his mom.

He should keep some distance between him and Caryn. He wanted to settle down, have children, and that wasn't going to happen with Caryn—it would be too bizarre—so he should try to keep things simple between them, especially since they would be linked forever because of Kevin. James just wanted to prevent awkwardness in the future.

Or so he tried to convince himself, as he drove to see her anyway.

Seven

"**T**able eight is asking about you," Venus said to Caryn at the beverage station.

Distracted, Caryn checked her watch. Twelve-thirty. How was Kevin doing? She wished it was closer to two o'clock and she could call him. "What?" she said to Venus, her words finally registering. "Someone…? Who?"

"I don't know. I haven't seen him before. Dark hair, kind of muscle-bound."

Panic nipped at her. She looked for an escape route. They'd followed her. They wanted more money. Or maybe it was someone else. Maybe Paul had other debts…

She found her voice. "What'd you tell him?"

Venus frowned. "I said you were working a private party. Shouldn't I have?"

"No. I mean, yes, it's fine. I'll take a look."

She peeked around the corner. James sat with a very attractive woman. Relief struck first, then…disappointment? A tiny twinge of jealousy, too, perhaps? James and the woman were talking and smiling, obviously relaxed with each other. She wore an engagement ring with a diamond large enough for Caryn to see from thirty feet away. She was attractive, too, with a long, thick braid down her back and a body like Caryn used to have before she lost so much weight.

Then it struck her. He shouldn't be here. He should be with Kevin.

What was she supposed to do now? She couldn't exactly march up to him and ask where her son was, not in front of the woman or the other customers. Not to mention that Rafael was in a foul mood. She didn't dare do anything to put her job in jeopardy.

If this was James's way of getting even with her for not telling him who she was when they first met…

But he'd been attracted, too. He'd invited her to dinner *before* he knew who she was.

Men. Games. To heck with— What was she thinking? She was not jealous.

"Tell him I said hello," Caryn said to Venus. She flipped through her order pad, double-checked the drink orders against what she'd put on the tray, then tucked her pad into her pocket and lifted the tray, positioning it on her shoulder and distributing its weight. She could avoid him easily enough, could find the patience to contact Kevin first. Maybe he'd decided against meeting the woman. "Oh, and also tell him that I recommend the poached salmon."

"But the salmon is—" Venus stopped. Her eyes sparkled. "Is he an ex-boyfriend? You want to get even with him for something?"

"Something like that." Okay, so maybe she was a tiny bit jealous, but as quickly as that thought came, she shoved it aside. She had work to do.

Caryn headed to the private dining room. As soon as she served the drinks and took the food orders from the women celebrating the end of a golf tournament, she would sneak into the locker room for just a few seconds and call Kevin.

But when she emerged from the dining room she found James waiting by the door.

Her irritation had escalated as the minutes ticked by. "What are you doing here?" she demanded, harsh and low, looking around for Rafael. "Where is my son? Why aren't you with him?"

The door to the private dining room hit her in the back as it opened. "I beg your pardon," a woman said.

"No, I'm sorry," Caryn said, moving aside. The woman kept walking toward the restroom. Caryn fired a furious look at James.

"I came specifically to tell you," he said calmly, his brows raised as if surprised by her anger. "Kevin and my mother hit it off, which is a mild term for the instant connection they made. Anyway, they didn't want me around."

Jealousy—a different sort—hit in full force now. She had enough to be worried about with James, now his mother…

"Me, too," he said, his gaze softening.

"You, too, what?"

"I was jealous that they found such quick common ground."

"I'm not—" She stopped. Blew out a breath. "I should be glad."

"That's what I told myself, too. Listen, I won't keep you. I just wanted to let you know what was going on."

"Thanks." Who is the woman you're with? she wanted to ask.

He turned back. "So that's the famous Venus who's waiting on us?"

Caryn nodded.

"I can see why Kevin is bewitched."

"Just what I needed to hear."

He laughed quietly.

She held up her order pad. "Gotta run."

"If you get a free minute, stop by my table. I'd like to introduce you to someone."

"If I can. I'm pretty busy."

He didn't reply for a few seconds, then said, "Venus said you recommend the poached salmon?"

Caryn faced an ethical dilemma. She couldn't tell him how mediocre the salmon was, without making Venus seem idiotic, that she'd told him the opposite of what Caryn had recommended.

"I don't like fish," he added. "Can you suggest something else?"

Dilemma solved. "Pot roast, if you like hearty."

"Yeah. Thanks."

She waved over her shoulder as she headed to the kitchen and turned in the sixteen lunch orders. She offered a smile of sympathy to the head chef, silently acknowledging his hard work, knowing that getting on his good side would result in less stress for her and the potential to make more money in better tips. It was one lesson she hadn't had to teach Venus, who was naturally accommodating to everyone. Even the dishwashers tripped over their feet to help her.

Caryn took eight salad plates from the refrigerator and

prepared the side salads, then ladled three bowls of clam chowder. It took that long for her to ponder why James was eating at the club. Was he a member? He must be or he wouldn't be allowed in. Unless the woman was. She did look athletic...

"Caryn." Rafael came up beside her. "Do you need a reminder of the rules?" He didn't try to keep his voice down, but almost shouted above the kitchen noise.

"Excuse me?"

"I made an allowance already today for your son to talk to you during working hours. Then you took advantage by conversing with that guest, Mr. Paladin. You know that's not allowed."

Caryn went rigid, but occasions like this demanded contrition, not explanation. "I'm sorry. It won't happen again."

He walked away. She'd never been reprimanded for any infraction before. Her face burned. Her conversation with James hadn't even lasted a minute. And she hadn't approached him, but vice versa, although she couldn't tell Rafael that, could she? What was she supposed to have done? Be rude to the customer?

She fixed a smile on her face and served the soup and salad, refilled the bread baskets, then checked the beverage station again while she had a few minutes before the entrées were ready. She had no outlet for the emotions tumbling riotously inside her—about Kevin, about James, his mother and now the criticism by her manager. She'd thought her life had settled in and settled down. Apparently she wasn't to be allowed that luxury.

Because she couldn't stop herself, she glanced at James and his companion. He angled his head and raised his brows expectantly, as if inviting her to the table. She turned away, dangerously close to tears.

"Are you okay?" Venus asked from just behind her.

"Sure." She grabbed a cloth and wiped down the outside of the soda dispensers.

"Do you want help serving when the entrées are up?"

"Rafael will assign who helps. But thanks." She walked away before Rafael, who seemed to see and hear everything, even if he wasn't in sight, caught her. Knowing she couldn't slip away to call Kevin before his two o'clock class frustrated her even more, but she couldn't take any chances. Not today. So, she wouldn't know what happened until he got home after five.

All because of James.

Oh, get real, she told herself. She wasn't mad because Rafael had chewed her out. She was mad because James hadn't told her he had a…fiancée, apparently.

And why should that bother her? It made her life much less messy, if James wasn't available for a relationship other than what he built with Kevin. Granted, she would welcome James into her life if Kevin wanted her to, but beyond that there wasn't a reason to learn more about each other.

Easy come, easy go.

"Who was the waitress?" Cassie asked James as they headed to their cars after lunch.

"Her name tag said *Venus*."

"Not the America's Sweetheart, Jamey. The other one. The redhead with the short hair and red lipstick."

"You don't miss much."

"I'm not supposed to miss much."

They reached Cassie's car. "Her name is Caryn Brenley."

"Brenley?" Her voice pitched higher. She grabbed his arm. "You found your child?"

"He found me. Well, she did, actually. His mother. Then he did."

"A boy."

"Yeah."

"How do you feel?"

"I don't know yet. Honestly, Cass. It's still confusing."

"Why?"

"Long story, and we both need to get back to work."

She unlocked her car but didn't open the door. "When did you meet him?"

"Saturday."

"And you're just now telling me?"

"I called. You weren't home. Then I realized I needed to let it sink in first."

"The mom's pretty. Awfully thin, though."

"She's been dealing with a lot over the past year."

"How about your old friend, her husband?"

"Died a year ago. Listen, I'll catch you up on everything, but not now."

Cassie cocked her head. "Why'd you bring me here with you?"

"I wanted to tell her something, and to watch her in action, frankly. I didn't think I should be sitting there alone—it would be too obvious. I hadn't counted on her not working the dining room." He looked back at the building. "I think she's upset with me for coming."

"Well...yeah."

"Why do you say it like that?"

"It's her place of business. You intruded. She probably has rules forbidding mingling with the customers. Every place I waited tables had a similar rule. Not that we always obeyed it."

Why hadn't he considered that? He looked toward the dining room windows, could see people still sitting at tables. Had he caused a problem for her?

"I can't go back and ask," he said to Cassie. "If she's in trouble for it, I would only make it worse."

"You'll figure out something." She hugged him. "I'm so happy for you."

"Don't be happy yet. There's a lot to work out between the three of us."

"It'll be worth the effort." She stepped back then opened her car door. "You coming into the office today?"

"Right behind you."

He waited until she backed out before he walked back to where his car was parked, closer to the building. He looked into the window again and saw Caryn standing there, looking back. He lifted a hand. She turned away.

Unpredictable. Why the hell had he thought he would like that about her?

Shortly after five o'clock James parked in front of Caryn and Kevin's three-story duplex. On the left side of the building, on the second floor, above a two-car garage, were two red-painted doors with different house numbers, one door leading to the downstairs unit, James assumed, and the other to the upstairs. Caryn lived upstairs.

He hadn't called ahead, deciding to take his chances rather than be turned down. Now he wondered whether to wait in his car for Kevin to get home and greet him before he went inside his house, or to knock on the upstairs unit and see if Caryn was there. He needed to talk to both of them, but not necessarily together. And just because Kevin got out of class at five o'clock didn't mean he would come straight home—which made James's decision for him. He would ring Caryn's bell.

She didn't keep him waiting, but didn't look surprised, either, so maybe she'd seen him coming.

"Hi," he said, in a moment of rhetorical brilliance.

She crossed her arms. "Hi."

Obviously she wasn't going to make this easy on him. "I came to apologize."

"For what?"

"For disturbing you at work. Did you get in trouble?"

"Yes."

He winced. "I'll fix it."

"No, thank you."

"But—"

"It wouldn't help, trust me on that. Is that it?"

Startled, he didn't say anything for a few beats. "No, that's not it. I'd like to talk to you, to get to know you. How about inviting me in?"

"I have company."

He was caught off guard. A boyfriend? He hadn't considered that possibility, probably because of the way she'd followed him that night, and the attraction she'd admitted to.

"Venus is here," she said into his silence.

He had no right to feel relieved, but he did. "Then maybe this is a good time. I should check her out a little more thoroughly so that I can advise Kevin properly."

Her lips twitched in an obviously reluctant smile. "She thinks you're an ex-boyfriend of mine."

"Why does she think that?"

"It's what I told her."

"Why—"

"My point is, you can come in, but I don't want you telling her what our relationship is."

"She won't think it's strange that an ex-boyfriend would show up and be let in?"

"She'll be curious. I have no problem with that."

"Your call." He followed her up the stairs and into a roomy living room with large windows overlooking the street. Her furnishings had probably come from her house; the rustic style suited a horse ranch, although it was not out of place here. She obviously had an eye for decorating, as the colors and accessories blended and complemented— words he'd learned from his decorator.

"Well, hi," Venus said coming into the room from what appeared to be the kitchen. She looked back and forth between Caryn and James.

"You already know each other," Caryn said.

"Not his first name."

"James," he said, extending a hand. "Jamey, if you prefer." He realized that Caryn never called him by his first name and wondered about it.

"You used to date?" Venus asked.

"We go way back," Caryn said, her smile wry. "Have a seat. Would you like something to drink?"

"I'm fine," he said, sitting on her tan-colored sofa. He wasn't sure what to say in front of Venus, who sat at the other end of the sofa and tucked her legs under her. Both women had changed from their uniforms. Caryn into jeans and a sweatshirt amazingly free of anyone's logo, and Venus into jeans and a soft pink sweater that made her look like cotton candy.

"I'm home!" Kevin called out, cutting through the tension in the room. James could almost hear a collective sigh of relief.

Footsteps bounded up the stairs, then the boy appeared. Three entirely different expressions crossed his face when he spotted each person in the room. His mother hadn't taken a seat yet, so he saw her first and grinned. Then he saw Venus and took a step toward her, then he came to an abrupt stop when he realized James sat on the same sofa.

If it hadn't been so awkward, it would've been funny.

Almost as one, everyone looked to Caryn.

Eight

The silence felt like a vise crushing Caryn. What had she been thinking, letting James in while Venus was there? *No one* could talk freely. Caryn wanted to talk to Kevin. Kevin would rather talk to Venus. Venus looked like she had questions for James. And James seemed to want to talk to everyone—and no one. Plus there was something different about him. She couldn't put her finger on it.

Kevin took charge. "You wanna come downstairs for a while? Listen to some tunes?" he asked Venus.

"Sure." She looked thrilled, in fact, to leave Caryn's apartment.

Caryn didn't blame her. She wanted to know how things went with James's mother, though. "Everything work out okay?" she asked her son.

His gaze shifted to James then back. "Great. Really great. I'll tell you later."

"Before you go, Kevin," James said, standing. He pulled a business card from the pocket of his shirt, the same plaid shirt he'd worn at lunch…with that woman…who wore the diamond engagement ring.

Caryn had temporarily forgotten that detail.

He passed the card to Kevin. "Your mom said you were looking for work. This guy's a friend of mine. He'll be around until ten o'clock tonight, if you're interested."

Kevin read the card. His eyes went wide. "Can I go right now?" he asked.

"You might want to change into something appropriate for a job interview," James said.

"A suit?"

James smiled. "No. A clean and ironed shirt would be good, though. And a less ratty pair of jeans."

"What's the job?" Caryn asked, feeling like a fifth wheel. She'd known James would take over. Known it without a doubt. He had that kind of pushy personality.

Kevin showed her the card. "A shooting range. How'd you know that's something I like?" he asked James.

"Thank your mom. She told me."

Kevin hugged her, then he hurried out of the room, Venus on his heels. She'd been silent during the entire exchange. Caryn wondered what she thought—that they were all crazy?

The downstairs door banged shut, followed by Kevin's door. They could hear his voice filtering through the floor, the words indistinct but the tone overrun with excitement.

"Thank you," she said to James. "I haven't seen him that happy in— Well, you know how long."

"It's up to him now."

"You're not paying your friend to hire him, are you?"

He smiled slowly, an utterly sexy, irresistible— No. Totally resistible. He apparently had a fiancée. Caryn had watched them laugh and talk, their heads close, then they'd hugged in the parking lot. She'd seen it and tried to ignore the twinges it brought.

"Wouldn't have occurred to me to subsidize him," James said. "It's hard to get a first job. All I did was provide a possibility. Caryn—" he moved a little closer "—I really am sorry you had trouble at work because of me. If Cassie hadn't set me straight, I would still be ignorant of what I'd done. You should've said something."

"Cassie?"

"The woman I wanted you to meet. We work together."

Did that mean they weren't a couple? They'd hugged. Male and female coworkers didn't usually hug. "She's very attractive," Caryn ventured.

"She's scary."

"What do you mean?"

"A highly competent investigator, and almost fearless. But not reckless, which is a good thing. She got engaged about a month ago. I wonder how long she'll stay in the business. She loves kids. I figure she'll get pregnant on her wedding night—or make a valiant effort, as much as she wants a kid of her own."

Caryn's relief took a nosedive, rooting her in place. She hadn't let herself acknowledge precisely how attracted she was to James until that moment—that moment when she thought he belonged to someone else.

Although he still might belong to someone else, for all she knew.

"You didn't," James said, then hesitated. "You didn't think Cass and I were a couple, did you?"

"Of course not." She turned away and headed for the kitchen without knowing why, except that she didn't want him to see the truth on her face.

"You did," he said, following her. "I invited you to have dinner with me, Mysterious. And I didn't know you were Kevin's mother then, either. I was attracted—to you, the woman."

"Okay."

"Hey." He put his hands on her shoulder and turned her toward him. His gaze held hers captive. "I figure trust is a real issue with you, and I understand that. But believe me when I say if I'd been involved with any woman, I wouldn't have asked you out."

She had two choices, believe him or not. With him so close to her she realized what was different about him. His beard was gone. "You shaved," she said, touching his cheek without thinking. He was an incredibly handsome man....

He'd gone perfectly still and the world went silent. She saw nothing but his face, felt nothing but his closely shaven skin against her fingertips, heard his breath getting raggedy, breathed a scent she couldn't name—something all him, she supposed. Now if she could just taste...

He lowered his head, captured her lips in a kiss so sweet it was painful. Her eyes stung, her body ached. He didn't put his arms around her, though, or deepen the kiss but lingered gently, carefully, as if afraid she would break, then he pulled back and pressed his cheek to her hair.

"This is a really bad idea," he whispered against her temple.

"I know." But it had been so long since she'd been touched, so long since she'd been held and comforted. She'd handled everything alone. Selling the house, buying a new one, moving. Never mind the gangsters. "Would you hold me, please?"

His arms slipped around her. She tucked her face against his neck and savored him. Her ice-cold bones began to thaw. A sob rose. She tried to make a sound to cover it, tried to pull away. His hold tightened, not painfully but insistently.

"Don't be afraid," he said.

She wasn't, but how could she tell him that? He just felt good. Strong. Protective. "I'm sorry," she said, embarrassed. "I'm so sorry."

"Shh. It's okay." He stroked her hair.

"I've just been…"

"Alone. I know."

After a minute she eased back. "Thank you," she said, turning away and going to the refrigerator, giving herself something to do. "I'm going to have some iced tea. How about you?"

"That'd be fine, thanks." He sat at the kitchen table. When she joined him with the drinks he said, "I checked on Paul's motorcycle. It was taken to a recycling yard months ago. The tow yard said you signed a release to the insurance company."

"I signed a lot of papers in those days. I don't remember one document from the rest."

"I can take a trip down there, see if I can track it down."

"Only if you think it will help. I assume it had been examined thoroughly."

He took a sip of his tea, then set down the glass carefully. She figured he had something important to say but was hesitant to say it. He looked different clean shaven. She'd kind of liked the bad-boy scruffiness after she'd gotten used to it. He looked…*nicer* now. Not as risky. It should've quieted her adrenaline, but no such luck. If anything, a lot of excess hormones were pole-vaulting inside her.

"Did Kevin find anything in Paul's paperwork?" he asked.

"I don't know. We haven't talked about it yet."

The front door opened, and Kevin raced up the stairs. "Mom?"

"In the kitchen," Caryn called out, grateful he hadn't caught them kissing. She didn't know how she could possibly explain that.

He shot into the kitchen. "Do I look okay?" He ran his hands down his long-sleeved, navy-blue dress shirt, patted his yellow and blue tie. His gaze flicked from Caryn to James, who nodded.

"You look nice," she said. "You'll need names and addresses and phone numbers for references."

"Like who?"

"Adults who would sing your praises," James said.

"It isn't enough that you recommended me?"

"You'll have to fill out an application like everyone else. It's one of the questions."

"I'll write down some names for you," Caryn said, standing. She realized she would be leaving them alone. She didn't want them to talk about James's mother—or anything else—without her. "Where's Venus?"

"Downstairs. I'm going to drop her at her house on my way."

"Good." She left the room, tracked down her address book then hurried back. She needn't have worried. They didn't seem to have spoken while she was gone. She wondered why, though.

"Tell me about your—James's mother," she said as she grabbed a pen and paper.

His eyes lit up. "She's cool. Did you know she sailed from San Francisco to Australia?" he said to James. "Just her and your dad."

"As a matter of fact, I did." He smiled. "It was the first year of their marriage. She was a few months pregnant with me at the end of it. They never stopped going on adventures, either. I've never been on the jungle ride at Disneyland, but I've been down the Amazon. And on safari, twice."

"Wow."

"I didn't really appreciate all they showed me until I was old enough to realize not everyone took those kinds of vacations."

"Your dad was a cop."

"Yeah. A good one."

Caryn heard pride in his voice.

Kevin leaned against the counter, relaxing. "Your mom showed me pictures." He nodded a little, as if to himself, as if coming to a decision. "I'm gonna go back another time when I don't have to be somewhere else."

"If you get this job," Caryn said, "you probably won't have much free time."

"I'll manage." He'd gone rigid. His tone was defensive.

"It was just a comment, Kevin."

"Whether you like it or not, Mom, I'm an adult. I can figure things out by myself now."

The silence that followed was one step short of torture. She finished writing down names and contact information and passed the sheet to her son. "Good luck," she said as cheerfully as possible.

"Thanks." He left without saying goodbye, which probably meant he was embarrassed by his own behavior.

"I'm sorry," she said to James, then picked up her glass, giving herself something to do. "I never know how he's going to react to anything these days. Pretty unpredictable."

"Unpredictable, huh?" He grinned, but she didn't know why. "Eighteen's a tough age. You want to break free from your parents, but you aren't necessarily ready to handle everything on your own yet."

"I admit I've had a hard time letting him go."

"Understandable, given your own loss. He seems like a good kid, though, with a good head on his shoulders."

"I hope so." She spun her glass on the table, then dragged her finger through the water beading up on the Formica surface. What now? Did he want to leave? Stay? Have dinner? Talk?

She tested the waters. "Would you like to see pictures of him growing up?"

A few beats passed. "Yes, I would. Thank you."

The emotion in his voice startled her. She hadn't tried to examine how he felt about everything—Kevin. Her. He'd known all these years that he had a child, of course, but had he wondered about him as a father might? She'd read articles written by other sperm donors. Some felt an attachment, a wish they could see the child, but most said they divorced themselves from the actuality of another human being, genetically theirs. They had helped someone who would've otherwise not been able to have a child. That was it. Like a civic duty.

She wanted to ask James where he stood, how he felt, but she wasn't sure she was ready for his answer. If he wanted to take Paul's place—

"Caryn?"

She lifted her head. "Hmm?"

"Pictures?"

She went to get her photo albums, then they spent the next hour poring over them. She shared stories of Kevin she'd forgotten but was reminded by the snapshot images. By default James also got a glimpse into her marriage and their family life—and so did she.

If anyone had asked her at any point during the past twenty years if her marriage was happy, she would've said yes. Certainly they had problems, like any other couple, but they'd worked through them. No marriage is perfect all the time.

But looking at the photographs gave her a different perspective. As time went by, she and Paul stood farther and farther apart, instead of arms wrapped around each other, as they had in the first few years. Again, normal, she supposed, for a settled-in relationship. There were fewer pictures as time went by, too. Also normal.

In the first ten years or so they'd worked hard, never having time or energy to be tired of each other or argumentative. They focused on surviving. Yearly his worth went up in the stuntman community. He made more money, enough for her to stay home with Kevin at what seemed like a critical time—prepuberty. She missed the company of neighbors in the isolated area where they lived. She no longer had coworkers, or praise for a job well done, or raises. Paul gave her a household allowance. Other than that, she knew nothing about their finances.

As she'd gotten to the album of Kevin's high school years, she saw changes in Paul that she hadn't seen in person. He'd lost weight. He looked gaunt. Worried? Scared? Had the gambling started that long ago?

"Caryn?" James asked.

She'd been staring at one of the last pictures she'd taken of her husband. *What a waste, Paul. What a total waste.*

"I'd like to take you out to dinner," James said, breaking into her consciousness.

She turned to look at him, this man who'd been a part of her life without being a part of her life for so many years. His strength was evident—physically and mentally. If he were anyone other than who he was, she would go after him—no, she would let him come after her. She smiled a little at the old-fashioned thought. But he was who he was.

Still, she needed to know the man who would hold a starring role in her son's life.

And she had to eat, didn't she?

Nine

"**W**here have you been?" Kevin demanded from the top of the stairs when James and Caryn returned from dinner later.

"We got a bite to eat," James said easily, before Caryn jumped into the fray and an argument ensued. Everyone was tense enough already, and Kevin's tone of voice indicated his readiness to let off some steam.

"You didn't leave me a note," he said, glaring at his mother.

"I figured we'd be back before you knew we were gone," Caryn said, moving past him. "How'd the interview go?"

James saw him relax, the abrupt change typical of a teenager.

"I got the job."

"Honey, that's wonderful!"

"Yeah. I'll just be doing stuff like cleaning up, but they'll give me more to do as I prove myself. I start tomorrow. I'll be working a lot of nights, and if nothing much is happening, I can do homework." He looked at James. "Thanks."

"You're welcome. I use that range, so I'll probably run into you now and then."

"You carry?"

"I was a bounty hunter for twenty years. I'm a P.I. now. What do you think?"

"I figure you don't trust anyone."

"Pretty close." They moved into the living room and were seated. He'd intended to just drop Caryn off and leave, but he didn't want to lose the opportunity to spend time with both of them. "How'd you do on going through your father's papers?"

"I can't believe how much crap he saved. I don't think he threw out anything."

"So, it's going to take you a while to sort it?"

"Yeah. Especially now that I've got a job, too. But I'll get it done," he added in a rush. "You don't need to do anything."

"I hadn't planned on offering."

"Okay. Well, I'm trying to put it in piles as I go. I think a lot of it can be tossed. He even saved utility bills from when he and Mom first got married. Crazy."

"I'm going to get a glass of water," Caryn said, standing. "Can I get either of you something to drink?"

James and Kevin shook their heads. James knew his unspoken assignment. He and Caryn had talked about it over plates of spaghetti and meatballs. He was supposed to ask about Venus. He waited until Caryn was out of sight, then he leaned forward and said quietly, "So, what's with you and Venus? Got something going?"

Kevin didn't answer. James figured he'd made a huge tactical error, which Kevin then confirmed. He leaned back, crossing an ankle over a thigh. "That's really none of your business, is it?"

How could he backpedal out of this one? "No. Not at all. I just noticed something between you and was curious."

For a moment Kevin looked as if he would give in and ask a question, then he changed his mind. "Actually, Emmaline gave me some hints."

So much for getting closer to the boy. At least his mother had. One step in the right direction.

"Venus did ask about you, though," Kevin said.

"Asked what?"

Caryn returned with her water.

"She wanted to know how long ago Mom and you had dated, 'cause she didn't think Mom had dated at all since Dad died."

James studied Caryn, whose expression gave away nothing.

"What did you tell her?" Caryn asked.

"Nothing."

"Good," Caryn said. "Because all I told her was that I'd dated James a couple of times right after we moved here but that it hadn't worked out. I didn't meet Venus until she was hired at GGC, a month ago."

"I did sorta let it slip that you're a P.I.," he added.

"Why did you do that?" Caryn asked. "You shouldn't have—"

"It's okay," James interrupted. "It doesn't matter." It did matter, but he didn't need Kevin feeling guilty about it. Like most people, Kevin found James's occupation fascinating. James didn't blame him for letting it spill to Venus.

He decided it was time to leave. "I think I'll head home," he said, standing.

Caryn stopped him. "I was hoping you could tell us about how you knew Paul."

She'd asked him at dinner, but they had decided to include Kevin in the conversation. "Okay, sure." He sat. "We met in high school. We played football together. I can't say we were best friends—we ran with different crowds most of the time—but we got along. We became better friends when we started college and found we were both criminal justice majors. Like you," James added with a smile at Kevin.

"Except my dad didn't do anything with his degree."

"What are your plans?"

"I don't know for sure. Cop, maybe. Lawyer. Who knows?"

A P.I., perhaps? James didn't ask the question. "In March of our sophomore year, my father's best friend was arrested for attempted murder. My dad believed his friend, also a cop, was innocent, that he'd been set up. Dad posted bail and secured it with his own house as collateral. The guy skipped. It was pretty humiliating for my dad, not to mention what it did to him financially."

"You went after the guy," Kevin said, as if knowing exactly how James felt at the time—angry for his father.

"Yeah. And I talked your dad into going with me, although it didn't really take much talking. We didn't tell our families what we were doing. Stupid." He shook his head at the memory. "But that's what we were, young and stupid. We made huge, amateur mistakes, except that we did locate him after two weeks of hunting him. Trouble was, this guy was not only smarter and more experienced than us, of course, he had more motivation for not being caught."

"He really was guilty of the attempted murder?" Kevin asked.

"Yes. And only sorry that he hadn't been successful."

"You and Paul didn't call anyone when you located him, did you," Caryn said, certainty in her voice. "Not your dad. Not the local police. You went after him yourself."

"We figured we could handle him. Two against one. You know. The invincibility of youth."

"And the felon had years of cop training behind him," she said, guessing. "And probably a gun."

James nodded. "I went after him first, and got shot in the shoulder. Paul lunged. He knocked the gun away. They fought. During the fight—" James looked at Caryn, then straight at Kevin "—your dad took a blow to the crotch."

"He was shot…there?" Horror filled Kevin's eyes and voice.

"Not shot. Guy kicked him, with steel-toed boots. Still Paul managed to knock him out before passing out from the pain. I tied the guy up with our belts, then called the cops. We were in Nevada, which complicated everything. There was the extradition back to California, not to mention how much trouble we were in from our parents and the local authorities and the San Francisco authorities *and* the bounty hunter sent to find the guy. He would've, too, within the hour."

"So," Caryn said carefully, "you gave your sperm as payback for him helping you?"

"Because the injury he received caused bleeding, which resulted in permanent damage to the sperm production mechanism—and because it was my fault he was there to begin with. He never told you that?"

"He only said he was infertile."

"Too much information," Kevin said, putting his hands over his ears, shoving himself up. "I gotta go."

He flew down the stairs. The door shut with a solid thud. A long silence ensued. "Maybe we should've talked first, after all," James said. "You could've told me what to tell and what not to."

"He needed to hear it. I hope knowing how headstrong you and Paul were, and the results, will make him think twice before he takes any chances himself."

"Yet you don't want to tell him the truth about Paul's gambling."

"That's different." She stared toward the stairway. "I forgot to ask more about his visit with your mother."

"I stopped by to see her before I came here. She said they had a terrific time together, that Kevin was 'very sweet.'"

"He's a good kid, most of the time. Listen, James, I need to ask your opinion on something."

Yes, I think you're pretty. Yes, I'd like to kiss you again. Hold you again. "What's that?"

"I didn't give Kevin every box of paperwork. I have three that are filled with the most incriminating files. I'm not sure what to do with them."

"I'll look through them, if you don't mind, then we can talk about whether to include Kevin. I'll pick them up tomorrow night, since he'll be working. You can let me know." He stood. "By the way, Caryn, I don't think you have to worry about Kevin and Venus as yet."

"Really?"

"He implies not."

"That's enough to make you believe it?"

"For now." He headed to the staircase, because he

wanted to stay. "And you don't have to walk me to the door," he added when she stood, too.

She followed him anyway, at least to the top of the stairs. "You okay?" he asked.

She nodded.

"Not sure if you want me in your son's life?"

"I'm sure. He needs you. I see that."

"Not sure about yourself?"

"I wouldn't say that."

"What would you say?"

"Nothing. Yet."

He smiled. "You surprise me a lot, Mysterious."

"Good."

His gaze dropped to her mouth, to her red lips. "Is it easier for you to call me than for me to call you?"

"Probably. If you answer your cell phone, no matter what, because I never know when I'll be given a break."

"It's rare that I can't answer it, but it happens."

"I'll try, then."

She'd lost that fragile look from earlier in the evening, and the I'm-tired-of-being-alone undertone to her voice. He didn't mind her needing him a little, but even more he liked the strength and capability he saw. "Good night."

"Night."

He didn't exactly tiptoe down the staircase, but he didn't hurry, either, although the wood creaked under his weight. When he pulled the door shut behind him, he noticed she wasn't standing and watching, waiting for him to leave. She'd walked away.

He grinned.

He sat in his car for a few minutes, listening to his voice mail on both his cell and home phone answering machine, in case he needed to return an urgent call. If he hadn't been taking care of business, he wouldn't have seen Venus knock on Kevin's door—and Kevin pull her in fast then stick his head back out, looking up and down the street before shutting the door.

Nor would he have seen, seconds later, their silhouettes against the downstairs curtains. No one could say she was keeping her distance.

Ten

Caryn drove home after work the next day, showered, changed into a flowy blue skirt and soft white cotton T-shirt, loaded the three boxes of paperwork into her car, then headed for James's house. She'd called him during her lunch break. Even though Kevin would be at work, they'd decided to meet at James's house. He'd told her to come over whenever she was ready.

She wondered how much work time he'd lost in the past week because of her and Kevin. James was on her mind most of the time, and it was hugely distracting. Was he distracted, too? She didn't think that was a good thing for someone in his line of work.

He must have been watching for her, because he came down the steps as soon as she parked.

She liked his smile.

"Boxes in the back?" he asked.

She nodded. There was something different about him today, but what? He wore jeans and a plaid shirt, the sleeves rolled up a few turns. He was still clean-shaven. She didn't think he'd had a haircut since last night.

"What?" he asked, his arms loaded down with two large boxes.

She'd been staring at him. She couldn't imagine what he'd seen in her expression. Then it struck her what was different. She'd kissed him—or he'd kissed her. She was looking at him through different eyes. Not as the mother of a child they shared biologically, but as a woman. A hungry woman. A needy woman. She'd been waiting for him to kiss her hello, when there was no real expectation of that. Last night was just…a fluke.

"What?" he repeated, an edge to his voice this time.

She smiled—because she felt good just being there with him. She could lie to herself and say it was nice to be able to share the responsibility of Kevin with someone else again, but it wasn't the only truth. Far from it.

"Nothing," she answered.

His brows lifted. "Nothing?"

She shrugged.

"Unpredictable," he muttered then headed up the stairs. "You wanna grab the other box, please?"

She got the smaller box from the car, then set the alarm and followed James. *Jamey.* Even though he seemed to want her to call him that, she didn't think it suited him. He was a James—calm, steady, reliable. Which was at odds with the risk taker she knew must be part of his makeup.

She followed him into his office. He took the box from her and set it on top of the other two. She wondered if he knew how hard it was for her to let him see the paperwork that proved Paul was a gambler, and not a very good provider. He would see everything about their finances over the past few years, good and bad. Her life would be bared.

Caryn looked at the boxes. She'd given him everything except one letter. A letter Paul had mailed to his private mailbox the day before he died. A letter she'd been forwarded not long ago. She hoped James would investigate the accident, come to the same conclusion as the police, so that she could believe it, too, then she would destroy the letter. Maybe she should have before.

"You aren't inhabiting earth today," James said from close beside her.

She turned toward him. "Sorry."

He eyed her seriously, steadily. Her heart picked up speed.

"Did Paul have a copy of his high school yearbook?" he asked.

"I didn't come across one."

James pulled a book from the shelf behind him and flipped it open, then turned it around. She smiled at the picture of Paul at seventeen, dragged a finger across the photo.

"Cute," she said, "He didn't look that much different when we met, a couple of years after this. Where's yours?"

He flipped ahead to the Ps.

She leaned over the book. "No doubting Kevin's paternity, is there? The resemblance is remarkable. Do you have baby pictures?"

"I'm sure my mom does. I could take you to meet her, if you'd like."

"Not yet, thanks." She would let Kevin establish his relationship first, because his mattered the most. She rested a hand on the top box. "Would you like to go through these together?"

"No." A short, simple answer.

"Why not?"

"I'm handling the investigation as I would any job I'd taken on. I'll ask questions when I need to."

"How do you separate yourself like that?"

"It's easy." He glanced at the stack, as he had every few seconds.

"You're anxious to dig in." That he wanted to work instead of spend some time with her prompted a little envy in her.

He finally focused on her, his demeanor softening. "You look very nice, Mysterious."

She couldn't tell him how much she enjoyed her nickname, but she did. A lot. "Thank you."

"I hope you'll stay for dinner."

She had noticed a wonderful scent in the air when she first walked into the house. Before she answered, he moved an inch or two closer.

"We're going to be in each other's lives for a long time, Caryn. We might as well learn to be comfortable together."

She was comfortable—too comfortable—even as he invaded her personal space.

He laid a hand on her shoulder. "I already appreciate who you are," he said. "A good mother, a loyal and faithful wife, and a woman of her word. I know you struggle with sharing Kevin with me, and I admire you all the more for being gracious about it."

"You give Kevin things I can't. I won't deny him what you offer, even if it stings a little." She stood a little taller. "So, what's for dinner?"

"Pork roast, scalloped potatoes, green beans almandine and sourdough bread."

"Are you trying to fatten me up?" She knew she would be healthier with a little more weight. Maybe it had been a big turnoff for him, holding her skinny body.

"I like good food," he said. "And it's even better shared."

Good answer. "Okay. I'd love to join you for dinner."

"We've got about fifteen or twenty minutes until it's ready. Would you like something to drink? Wine? Tea?"

"White wine, thanks."

"Go take a seat in the living room. I'll join you in a minute."

The last time she'd been there, she'd noticed the room only as a way of distracting herself from the high-pitched emotion of the moment. What struck her now was how restful the room was. Music came from speakers hidden somewhere, classical, nothing she could identify. The fireplace looked ready to set a match to.

She'd just taken a seat on the sofa when James joined her, a glass of white wine in each hand. She murmured her thanks. He sat on the couch, too, although not next to her.

"I keep forgetting to ask you about your bike," she said.

"What you paid will cover the damages."

She wondered whether that was the truth, but she figured she would never know for sure. "Will you get it back soon?"

"The new fender needs to be chromed. Next week, I think." He laid an arm along the back of the sofa and angled toward her more. "Do you like your job?"

"It's okay."

"Something else you'd rather be doing?"

"I'm not trained for much else."

"No secret passion?"

Now *there* was a loaded question. She hid a smile behind her wineglass as she took a sip.

When she didn't answer, he questioned her further. "Obviously you like horses. Would you like to work with them again?"

"Are you running an employment agency for the Brenley family?" she asked, amused.

"I'm just curious."

"Okay. Well, I think I've had my fill of horses, except to ride now and then. Taking care of them and the stables was hard, physical work."

"Isn't waitressing hard?"

"Yes, but differently. My feet take the most abuse." She watched his gaze slide to her feet. She wore soft leather slip-ons, old and comfortable.

After a few seconds, he set down his wineglass, moved closer to her and picked up her feet.

She jackknifed forward, trying to pull free of his grasp but couldn't. "What are you doing?"

"Pampering you a little." He stared at her, almost unblinking, daring her with his eyes. Daring what? She swallowed. It had been so long since anyone had done anything just for her.

Well, why not give in? She let him lift her feet into his lap. He pulled off her shoes in a way that felt downright erotic, almost as sexy as if he'd undressed her. Oh, yes, it had been way too long. She closed her eyes and leaned back, then felt her glass being taken from her hand. She heard a soft tap as he put it on the coffee table.

He pushed a thumb into each instep. She drew in a hard, quick breath at the pain and pleasure his touch brought. Her fingers dug into the suede fabric. She relaxed them one at a time, then her hands, then her arms. He didn't speak. She wasn't sure whether she wanted the distraction of a conversation or not. Without it she focused on his touch, couldn't ignore it.

He had magic hands, slow, steady, sensational. He deepened the pressure, rotated her ankles, massaged each toe, found every sore spot and massaged it into mush. A sigh escaped her, although sounding embarrassingly like a moan. Except for a spa day at a salon that some of her girlfriends had arranged before she moved to San Francisco, no one had touched her for longer than a second or two, and nothing as intimate as what James was doing, even though his hands never strayed farther than her ankles.

Her body warmed on its own in reaction, his touch as arousing as if he were stroking her body. The denim fabric of his jeans under her calves abraded sensually. Her knee-length skirt had slipped back enough to expose her knees and a few inches of each thigh. She decided not to yank the skirt over her knees, not wanting him to know how much his touch affected her.

Maybe she shouldn't care. They were adults, with needs....

No. A lifetime connection awaited them through Kevin. Better to keep the relationship close but not intimate. They would share grandchildren at some point.

Grandchildren! She opened her eyes at the image.

"What's wrong?" he asked, but not taking away his hands.

A bell began to chime, a timer, she thought, as it didn't shut off. Saved by the bell. Dinner was ready.

His hands stilled, but he didn't take them away. Instead he curved them over her feet, keeping them warm. "What's wrong, Caryn?" he repeated.

Seeing him so close, feeling his legs under hers and his hands touching her bare feet, she didn't want to have to hold back. "I just realized we will probably share grand-children eventually."

James froze in place. Words stuck in his throat.

"Does that make you feel old?" she asked.

"Old" was the least of it, he thought. Considering he was looking forward to becoming a father, the idea of becoming a grandfather was almost beyond comprehension. "I do not feel old," he said. "And you don't look old enough to be a grandmother."

"Thank you. I don't think I'm ready for the pitter-patter of little feet at this point in my life, either. I'm just getting Kevin out of the house, if only downstairs, so far."

Something inside him shifted. The path to marriage and fatherhood made a sharp left turn. "A grandchild wouldn't live with you."

"One would hope not, anyway, but it happens. Regardless, I would be very involved. I know that about myself." She pulled her feet free, then stood and slid her feet into her shoes. "Thank you for the foot rub. Dinner is ready, I gather?"

Maybe it was safe to enjoy a more intimate relationship, after all, he thought. She wouldn't want marriage and children, but maybe she would be agreeable to more than friendship with him. It might complicate things later on, depending on how the relationship ended.

He would give it some thought….

He considered it all through dinner, even though they talked of other things, of Kevin and his childhood, of their own lives, of some of his funniest pursuit stories. She insisted on helping with dishes. Then the moment he shut the dishwasher he came to a decision. He wouldn't kiss her. Wouldn't take a chance that their lifelong relationship-to-come would be damaged by a short-lived affair, which it would have to be. She didn't want children. Plus, they had a child together already. That couldn't be acknowledged to the world in general. Enough strangeness existed in the relationship without adding to it. Why complicate it?

"I'd like to see your garden before I go," she said.

You're going already? It had been a long time since he'd enjoyed himself as he had over dinner. Maybe Cassie was right. Maybe he'd been aiming too young. There was something to be said for life experience.

The up lights he'd installed around the yard spotlighted elegant trees and a bed of mums in full bloom. They walked a winding path.

"This is so nice," she said, looking up at a liquid amber tree. "We used to have one of these," she said, walking toward it.

Along the way she dipped her fingers in a birdbath, and her smile turned into a grin.

He shook his head slowly, cautioning her, anticipating what she was about to do.

But she ignored his warning and flicked a few drops of water at him and ran. He threatened her, then caught up with her. They were both smiling.

She rested her back against the liquid amber, catching her breath, and reached up to pluck a leaf from a nearby branch. Her fingers worked at it, shredding it thoroughly, then she sprinkled the shreds over his head and laughed when he shook them off and onto her instead.

She was a dangerous woman when she smiled at him like that. He knew her life wasn't easy, that she'd suffered a lot, some of it needlessly because of Paul's gambling addiction, but she seemed to be moving on. He didn't want to do anything to hurt that process. But damn, when she looked at him as she was…

He brushed his hand over her head, dusting away the leaf bits. Then somehow he was cupping her face with one hand, then the other. He'd kissed her yesterday, but that was different. That was almost in sympathy. This would not be. Tell me if you want me to stop, he told her silently.

If she answered, it was silent, too. She lifted toward him. Her arms slipped around his waist. Their lips touched. Melded. Opened. She rose on tiptoe; he wrapped her in his arms to keep her steady…and close…and closer yet. Hints of mint-chocolate-chip ice cream flavored the kiss. What started cool, heated. Mint and chocolate gave way to destiny. There was no other way to describe how he felt, how she felt to him, how they felt together, as if they'd both been waiting for this moment since they'd created a life together anonymously all those years ago.

He angled closer, pressed her to the tree. His chest cushioned her breasts, which had nourished his son, their son. He slid his hands to her sides, his palms pressing the sides of her breasts. She stopped kissing him back, stopped moving, and waited instead, not breaking contact, but just waiting. He lifted his head, held her gaze, moved his hands until he covered her breasts, her nipples hard against his palms. After a moment she grasped his wrists. He stopped, but she shook her head, closed her eyes and used her hands to make his move.

Ahh. Permission. He watched her face transform with ecstasy as he toyed with her nipples through the lightweight T-shirt and flimsy bra. He slipped a leg between hers, pressed his thigh to the apex and reveled in the way she tipped her head back farther, her lips parted, a low, throaty sound more than hinting at her response. He nipped at her earlobe, dragged his tongue down her neck, under the neckline of her shirt. He caught her knee, dragged her leg up and alongside his. She drew a long, hissing breath as he moved his thigh in circles against her. She whispered his name. He closed his mouth over her breast, pulled lightly at the hard peak under the two layers of fabric.

Then she moved her hands, pressed them to his chest and pushed him back, not roughly but with determination.

"I can't," she said, panting, her forehead pressed to his.

"Can't what?"

"Do this. Us. It's so fast. There's so much to consider. Not just how good it would feel for now, for the moment. There's later…."

How good it would feel. He had no doubt it would feel spectacular. How she found the strength to stop amazed him. Her wholehearted response taunted him. He wanted to pleasure her, just to feel her go wild in his arms. He didn't care if he didn't…

"Just let me   " he kissed her, ran his tongue around her lips "—take care of you."

Her breath went raggedy. "I can't…let you…do that."

"Sure you can."

"But… what about you?"

"Another time, maybe. Let me, Mysterious. Please." Their lips were touching, breath mingling. The air was saturated with the scent of her arousal, a silent beggar demanding satisfaction.

"What would you do?" Her voice was hushed, her interest clear.

"Let me show you." He waited a few seconds. He would give her a preview of what they could have together, even if only for a little while. An affair to satisfy their curiosity and get that out of the way. Those questions would be answered, and their relationship could settle in without ever having to wonder what it would've been like to make love.

"You don't want to leave it like this."

"You're right. I don't want to, but I have to. I'm sorry."

He took a step back, not angry but surprised and disappointed.

"I should go," she said, hesitation turning her words almost into a question.

"Okay." He had to believe there would be another time, another opportunity.

"I'll see myself out," she said, before moving quietly through the yard and into the house. He roused himself from his stupor and followed her, arriving at the bottom of his front steps just as she pulled away from the curb. She waved. He just watched.

Then as he started back into the house he noticed a car parked nearby. Dark, two-door sedan, typical of cop undercovers. He saw the silhouette of a man inside. It struck James that the same car had been there earlier, when he'd come outside to greet Caryn—yet the guy hadn't followed her when she left a minute ago, a good sign. James walked close enough to see the license plate, then closer still to check out the man inside, who turned away as James approached. He kept walking, past the car to the newspaper rack at the corner. He bought a paper and headed back to his house.

Hours later the car pulled out.

In the morning it was back.

Eleven

James had a plan. He called Cassie, and she agreed to drive to his house, park out of sight of the stranger, then follow if he followed James. A direct confrontation would've suited him more, but would accomplish nothing except to hear a lie, probably, and tip the guy off that he'd been spotted. It was better to know who and where your enemies were.

Cassie reached James by cell phone when she arrived. Deciding that if he were a target of some sort, he would've been hit the night before, he went down to his garage and backed out his work car, as if nothing were different. He hit the speaker phone and dialed Cass's cell number as he headed up the street.

"He's not following you," Cassie said.

James could see that and was glad to be wrong, although he wondered who in the neighborhood was under surveillance, and by whom, and why. "Stay put for a few minutes. I'll come around and park behind you, then you can take off. I want to see what he's up to."

"Sure. How's every— Hold on. He's getting out of his car.... Jamey, he's opening your side gate. He's in your backyard."

James sped up. "Is he carrying anything?"

"Nothing I can see. I'll go for a little stroll in front of your house."

"Yeah, okay. You armed?"

"Yep."

He made the final turn that brought him back to his street, spotted a parking space and spent little time trying to park straight. He slammed the gearshift into Park and jogged toward his house, turning his cell phone to vibrate as he ran. With gestures only, he signaled Cassie to stand at the bottom of his steps, then he pulled out his gun, lifted the gate latch and crept into his yard until he could peer through some bushes at the back of the house.

A short, muscular man with a shaved head stood at James's back door, running his fingers around it, probably checking for a security system.

Baldy inched to a nearby window, peered in, then checked it for wires, too. To get him for breaking and entering, James had to be patient and let him do what he'd planned. The silent alarm would trigger a signal to a pager in James's pocket, which he'd already turned off, and at his office, which meant that his boss, Quinn Gerard, would come running, if he was there.

Baldy pulled a cell phone from his jacket pocket and appeared to punch a speed dial button. James picked up a word now and then but not whole sentences. He gathered that the guy was asking for advice. James heard the words *alarm* and *risk*. Then the cell phone was put away and he looked around the yard. James jerked back, out of sight. The sound of glass breaking followed. Baldy had broken in. The alarm was triggered, but he didn't know it yet.

James peeked around the corner again. The guy stood in place as if waiting for an alarm or a neighbor. When he decided enough time had passed, he reached through the broken glass on the back door and unlocked it. Glass crunched under his feet as he tiptoed into the house.

James followed.

He crouched as he ran under the windows then slipped silently into his house, scraping the glass bits from the bottom of his shoes before he stepped onto the kitchen floor. He swore silently. He hadn't let Cassie know he'd gone in. Bad move, going in without backup, even though he'd done it for years as a bounty hunter. He knew better. Too late now, though. At least she would be guarding the front.

Noise came from his office, the sound of paper being shuffled. He moved with his back to the wall, inching his way toward the room. When he reached the doorway he peered in. Baldy was stuffing Paul's papers into the boxes James had emptied last night. All that work, all the sorting James had done, was in shambles.

"Hands up!" James shouted as he entered the room, blocking the doorway, his weapon drawn.

Wearing his panic like a too-big overcoat, Baldy sought an escape route.

"Put the box down and your hands up," James said, making a point of aiming his gun at the man's heart.

Baldy bent over then suddenly heaved the box at James's midsection, spinning him around and almost knocking him over as the crook sped out of the room, adrenaline giving him extra speed and strength. James had no defensible reason to shoot him, so he went after him, lunging, catching him by the jacket and yanking, but the guy slipped out of the sleeves and kept going—through the kitchen, across the broken glass, out the back door, into the yard, over the fence.

James followed, but the guy was at least fifteen years younger, and he cleared fences in a single bound. He was long gone by the time James climbed the second fence.

He made his way to the sidewalk. Cassie spotted him and came running. Quinn pulled into his driveway. The gang was all there.

James hooked a thumb over his shoulder as Cassie reached him. "He does a helluva superhero imitation. He's gone."

"What's going on?" Quinn asked when he reached them.

"Let's go in the house." His ego stung, James led the way. He remembered why he'd gotten out of the bounty hunting business. He couldn't keep up with the young outlaws who could run faster and longer than he could. It struck him then that another six or seven years from now when his hoped-for child would want to play baseball with him, that he might not be able to. The thought depressed him further.

He caught Quinn and Cassie up to speed on Caryn and Kevin, and placed two calls—first to the police to report the break-in, then to arrange to have the glass in his back door replaced.

James scooped up the jacket he'd pulled off Baldy, found no ID but did find a cell phone.

Quinn got a plastic bag to preserve prints for a later check, then took it with him into the kitchen. "I'll deal with this."

"What do you think, Jamey?" Cassie asked. "Was the guy after this paperwork in particular or anything he could get his hands on?"

"My guess is he's connected to Caryn, or rather Paul, somehow."

"But she paid them off."

"Someone else he owed money to, maybe? Something altogether different? Baldy would've had to have been watching her place and saw her put the boxes in the car. How else would he know where to find them?"

"Baldy?"

"For lack of a another name," he said.

"Are you going to tell Caryn?"

"Yes." He rubbed his forehead. He wanted to sort through the papers again and really dig in now. There had to be something to give him a clue, something Caryn had overlooked.

"Does she need protection?" Cassie asked.

He'd been wondering the same thing. And if she was in danger, so was Kevin. And now that James had chased off Baldy, would they bring someone else in? Someone who would take more violent action?

"Maybe," he said to Cassie.

"You should move them in here."

Quinn stormed into the office. "Can't release that infor mation, my ass," he said, apparently to himself. "I need to use your computer."

James and Cassie smiled at his belligerence. Quinn was probably trying to get information on Baldy's cell phone by going through legal channels, something he'd been doing for only a year, since he'd become a legitimate P.I. instead of a shadow man who straddled legal and illegal as necessary to do the job. "Have at it," James said then turned to Cassie. "Baldy wasn't staking out Caryn."

"*This morning* he wasn't."

"Let's go take a look at the car," he said.

"It's a rental," Quinn said as he typed. "I already checked it out."

"Rented by John Doe?" Cassie asked.

"John Deer." He grinned. "The cleverness of crooks." His expression turned serious again as he searched for information.

"The only way I could get Caryn and Kevin to move in here is if Caryn told him the truth about his father's debts."

"It's a hard thing to find out about your father, but he's eighteen, Jamey. Maybe it'll be his ounce of prevention."

"Yeah." He looked around the room blindly. "I need to talk to Caryn. I need to make sure she isn't being targeted."

"Go," Cassie said. "I'll wait for the cops and the window guy. Give me your alarm code. We'll call when Quinn's done his magic and found out who owns the cell phone."

"Don't do anything you could lose your license over," James said after he wrote down the code for Cassie, then left.

He wished he had his bike, but he'd even turned in the loaner since that job was done.

After fighting traffic he finally pulled into the GGC parking lot and then walked to a spot where he could see into the dining room. He spotted Venus, who smiled and waved. He mouthed Caryn's name. In a minute she came to the window and held up both hands as if to say ten minutes. He went to the employee entrance to wait for her.

She was pulling on a sweater as she came through the door. He hadn't realized how chilly it was. His adrenaline heated him as if a dial was turned to high.

"What's wrong?" she asked. "Kevin—?"

"He's fine." James had already called him on a ridiculous pretext, had woken him up. James told Caryn what had happened.

She shivered, drew her sweater closer. "The same people, you think? Or different ones? There could be *more?*"

"I don't know yet. Cass and Quinn are working on it, too. We'll get to the bottom of it, I promise you that." Idly he rubbed her arms, trying to warm her. She continued to shake. "Caryn—"

"I don't like the sound of that."

"I haven't said anything."

"You're about to say something I'm not going to like."

"You need to tell Kevin."

"No."

"Yes. Because you and Kevin need to move in with me until we have answers."

She went rigid. *"No."*

"Yes." He loosened his hold as she tried to pull away. "I can't guarantee your safety, otherwise."

"What makes you so sure we're in any kind of danger?"

"I don't know for certain, *but I'm sure as hell not taking any chances.*"

Caryn jumped at his tone of voice, uncompromising and commanding, with maybe a little fear tossed in. He already felt responsible for her and her son.

His cell phone rang. She walked away from him as he talked. Move in with him? Tell Kevin? She dragged her hands down her face. Life was supposed to be settling down! she wanted to scream to the heavens.

"Caryn."

She spun around.

"That was my boss, Quinn. He says the cell phone belongs to a business in L.A. He's checking out the company, but it's probably a front for something."

"Was he able to trace his calls?"

"He can't do that. If he got caught trying—hacking— he'd lose his license. He'd have to go deeper than he did to get the ownership info, and it's a much higher risk to track numbers. Anyway, we had to call the police, and the D.A. can probably get the information."

"You called the police?"

"Of course I did." He gentled his tone. "It doesn't mean we stop investigating on our own." He touched her cheek.

She wanted to lean against him. To feel his arms around her. She was so grateful she wasn't dealing with this whole mess alone anymore. Still, she didn't want to tell Kevin, to ruin his memory of his father.

"Tomorrow is the one-year anniversary of Paul's death," she said.

James did sweep her into his arms then. Tears sprang, burned. She squeezed her eyes shut.

"Isn't it enough for him to deal with?" she asked. "The anniversary?"

"I'm sorry about the timing. But he needs to be told. For his own sake, he needs to be told."

She felt his lips graze her hair. His leather jacket smelled comforting, of all things.

He moved her back but didn't release her. "After your shift, you're off for the weekend, right? And no school for Kevin, either."

"His new job?"

"I don't think it's a good idea for him to be working where there are guns."

"He's going to be so upset."

"You have to help me make him see there's no choice. The job will be held for him."

"All right." What else could she say? "I'll talk to him this afternoon."

"*We'll* talk to him. I'll be in the parking lot when you're done with work and follow you home. Cassie will track down Kevin after his last class and follow him. You can't tell anyone. Not even Venus."

"Okay."

For a second she thought he was going to kiss her. Was it just last night he'd kissed her like there was no tomorrow? And just look what tomorrow brought....

"Everything will be fine," he said.

She tried to lighten the moment. "I bet you say that to all your..." She wasn't sure what word to use. Victims? Clients? Women?

"Friends," she finally said.

"You're more than a friend."

She stared at him. He cupped her face. "I don't know how that happened so fast, but it did."

"As Kevin's mother?"

"As my...Mysterious."

She swallowed. "That's kind of a big complication."

"No kidding." He brushed her lips with his, deepened the kiss slightly, then pulled her close as he changed angles.

The door opened against Caryn's back, startling her. He caught her arm, keeping her from falling.

"Oh, I'm so sorry," Venus said, her eyes shining. "I didn't realize.... I'll tell Rafael you need an extra minute." She disappeared.

"I have to go," Caryn said, angry at herself that she'd

forgotten where she was, worried as she was about Kevin, and confused and yet happy about James.

"I'll see you at three," he said.

She nodded, then slipped inside the building.

"Oooh," Venus said with a grin. "Hot stuff, huh? You're so cute together."

Caryn smiled, despite the uncertainties she faced. "Get back to work," she ordered Venus playfully.

"Yes, ma'am. Lovebird, ma'am."

Lovebird? No, not love. Not yet. But something powerful enough to allow her to trust him when she didn't think she would ever trust anyone again.

It felt good.

Twelve

James wasn't sure what kind of reaction he'd expected from Kevin but it wasn't silence, this absolute, total silence. Kevin had listened to Caryn's explanation, made eye contact with James as he'd added his perspective, then sat without saying a word.

Caryn caught James's eye and gave him a questioning look. He shrugged.

"Do you have any questions?" Caryn asked her son.

"No."

"You must have—"

"I don't, Mom. I'm trying to find a polite way to say I told you so. But polite doesn't matter now, does it? You waited too long, kept this a secret too long. There's no trail to follow. My father was murdered, and we could have found his murderer if you hadn't kept this a secret." He shoved himself out of the chair and stormed across his mother's living room. "Thanks for your faith in me. I told you something was wrong. I told you."

James couldn't even defend her well because he believed the same as Kevin, at least about telling, not that Paul had been murdered. He didn't have enough evidence to come to that conclusion yet. But he also understood Caryn's fear and what had driven her to keep the gambling and payoff to herself.

He saw Caryn's eyes well up, but she didn't argue the point.

"If they were as professional as they appear to be, you wouldn't have had a trail to follow then, either," James said to Kevin. "Give your mother a break. She did what she felt was necessary in order to keep you and herself safe."

"She should've called the cops."

"Maybe so."

"Look where we are now!" Kevin jammed his hands in his pockets. "We're going to have to hide out. I just got a job. I'll be fired."

"What's happening now may have nothing to do with what happened then," James said to Kevin. "We don't know it's the same people. Why would they get involved a year after the fact, especially since they've already been paid off? And as for your job, it's safe."

"For now."

"For however long it takes."

Kevin seemed to relax a bit at that. James watched Caryn lay her hands on her thighs and look at the floor, as if trying to will away overwhelming emotions by focusing on the rug. He wished he could put his arm around her. He wished he could take her to bed and give her something else to think about.

"You both need to pack enough clothes for a few days," he said instead. "Kevin, we'll take all your dad's paperwork along, too. You can work on it at my house."

"I haven't said I'll go."

"You'll—"

"It's the safest thing to do," James said, interrupting whatever Caryn was about to say. He couldn't force Kevin. She would try, as his mother, but she couldn't force him, either.

"You're trying to be my dad."

The belligerence in his voice hurt James, but he had to ignore it, excuse it. "I'm not. I'll be your friend, though. And I just happen to be equipped to handle this kind of situation. Frankly, Kevin, I could use your input. We've got a weekend. Let's take advantage of it."

"I have plans for tomorrow night."

Caryn's head came up fast at that. She gave James an accusatory look. He had, after all, said she had nothing to worry about. He hadn't told her he'd later seen Kevin and Venus through the curtains, embracing.

"You'll need to cancel them," James said. "Plus, you can't tell her what's going on."

"Who?"

"Venus."

"I didn't say I had plans with Venus. Other plans. What am I supposed to say?"

"That it's the one-year anniversary of your father's death," Caryn said quietly. "And we decided we needed to spend it together."

After a few seconds, Kevin approached her. "I didn't forget. I just wanted to be thinking about something else that day."

She grabbed his hand. "I completely understand that." She looked at James. "What if someone sees us leaving here with our suitcases? Or arriving at your house?"

"Pack your stuff in grocery sacks. After we leave, Cassie will pick up everything and bring it over later, as if she's delivering groceries. Not too many bags, okay?"

"There are a lot of boxes," Keith said.

"Sorted by year?"

"Not really."

"I'll work something out. For now, why don't you both get ready?"

Kevin headed to the stairs then stopped. "I should use the back stairs, don't you think? They lead to the yard, and there's a door into my kitchen from there."

James had just been about to suggest it. "Good idea."

"He's right," Caryn said after the back door shut. "I should've contacted the police."

"Hindsight. You were scared. What's done is done." He pulled out his phone and dialed Cassie as Caryn disappeared into her bedroom to pack. "Hey, Cass. We'll be ready in twenty."

"Quinn's here with me," she said. "We can drive over and walk the block. See what we can see."

"Thanks." He tucked the phone in his pocket and went to look out the front window. Because he was three stories up, he saw only the tops of cars. Who knew who sat inside, watching? He had to get Caryn and Kevin out of this house, into his car, then into his house without anyone seeing. And then he had to do the same thing with those boxes.

It was the least of his worries. He had no doubt he could protect them coming and going.

But just who was going to protect him from falling harder for both of them when they would be living with him?

In James's office later, Caryn concentrated first on organizing the papers from the three boxes that she'd given James, as Kevin took over the living room to sort what he had. James went back and forth between them. It was almost midnight. They'd been at it for hours. Caryn sat cross-legged on the floor. She was so tired, she was ready to let the papers be her mattress. But she couldn't. Not yet. She had to tell James something, but not until Kevin went to bed.

"Want to call it a day?" James asked from the doorway.

She nodded. Even the coffee she'd had an hour ago wasn't giving her a boost. "How about you?" she asked.

"I think we're organized. Tomorrow we can start to make sense of it all."

"Will you go to sleep or will you continue to work on—" she opened her arms "—all this?"

"I'm going to bed."

She wished she could climb in bed with him. Just to sleep beside him would make her feel better. Just to be held…

Which was a big, fat lie. Not that she didn't want to be held, but she wanted everything. To kiss and be kissed, to touch and be touched, to have the freedom to make love with him, to feel him over her, inside her. To forget about everything else.

"Caryn?"

"Hmm?"

He'd come close, was crouching in front of her. "Did you fall asleep?"

She smiled and shook her head. She reached to touch his hand—

"Mom."

She jerked her arm back. Her gaze flew to James's.

"He can't see," James whispered. "I'm blocking."

"What, honey?"

"I want to go to bed."

"We were just talking about that. I'll be right behind you." She accepted James's help to stand. She'd been sitting for so long, she stumbled. He caught her by the elbow.

"Whoa."

"Sorry. Foot's asleep." She shook it. Kevin had come up close and took her other hand. She let go of James's.

"I'll help you upstairs," Kevin said.

She laughed. "I'm not doddering yet. Just give me a minute." She didn't look at her son's face but at the floor and moved her foot around until the pins and needles went away, aware that James had stepped out of reach. Was Kevin jealous? He was certainly being proprietary. Or had he seen something between her and James? Something they weren't aware they were showing?

"Okay, I'm ready. See you in the morning, James. Thanks so much for putting us up and taking care of us."

"You're welcome."

She tried to give him a casual smile, but it felt forced now that she figured Kevin was watching closely.

"Night, Kevin," James said.

"Night." A lifetime of politeness drilled into him by his mother came with the single word.

She and Kevin climbed the stairs. She'd seen her assigned guest room only to unpack her clothing after Cassie brought the bags, and found it as beautiful as the rest of the house, with a delicate four-poster bed and rose-printed quilt. She couldn't wait to sink into the big, inviting bed.

She needed to stay awake long enough to talk to James, however. She would keep no more secrets from him.

"You okay here?" Kevin asked at her door.

"Sure. Why wouldn't I be?"

"This doesn't seem totally lame to you? Hanging with the guy who, you know."

"I'm just grateful he's in our lives at the moment. I don't think I could've handled another threat alone."

"You shouldn't have handled the first one alone." Accusation was in his voice, but not bitterly so.

"I realize that now."

"I can take care of you, you know. Dad would want me to."

"I know. It's nice to have help, though, don't you think?"

He shrugged. "It's okay."

She patted his cheek. "I'll see you in the morning." She turned toward her room.

"Mom?"

"Yes?"

"From the look on your face earlier, I'm guessing you don't want me to date Venus."

Not now, Kevin, she wanted to say. Not now. "Five years is a big difference at your age."

His jaw twitched; his face flushed red. "She...she doesn't have any more, you know, experience...than I do."

The fact he revealed such personal information about himself, as well as Venus, gave Caryn hope. She'd thought he'd stopped confiding in her. "I like Venus, Kev. She's a sweet girl. Just don't be in a hurry."

"Emmaline said the same thing."

The more Caryn knew of James's mother, the more she liked her. "I know your dad gave you the sex talk—"

"And the protection talk. You don't need to. Really. We're not…there, Mom. We're just friends." He hurried away then.

She didn't know whether to feel relieved or happy. Both, she guessed. She was going to have to let go of him. She could see he'd matured in the past year in ways she hadn't recognized. Time to remember that he was no longer a child, but fast becoming a man.

She put on her red flannel pajamas, yellow fleece robe and blue fuzzy slippers then looked in the mirror. Nope. Nothing sexy about that look. Her lipstick had faded away long ago. She hadn't replaced it and didn't now. She found the letter from Paul and tucked it in her pocket.

Then she sat on her bed to wait until the rest of the household slept.

James knew he was cheating by taking a stack of the papers to his bedroom instead of just going to sleep, but there was no way he would fall asleep, at least not for long, not while there was a threat to Caryn or Kevin.

The finances were complicated and not his forte. One of the ARC partners was married to a CPA, also an investigator in the firm. James would call first thing in the morning and see if she could fly up and take over that aspect of the investigation, even though it was Saturday. James was looking for anything unusual that jumped out at him. So far all he knew for sure was that Paul made a lot of money for the work he did, yet less than half went into the family bank accounts.

He piled the papers into stacks then carried them downstairs. On his way back to his room he put an ear to Kevin's door. Nothing. No sound. James had heard him talking earlier, probably on his cell phone to Venus, even though it was after midnight.

James moved on to Caryn's door. Silence from there, too. He leaned against the doorjamb, flattened his hand on the door. He liked having them there, liked knowing there were people in the beds. He would've liked it a whole lot more if Caryn had been sharing his room instead of sleeping alone.

On a whim he turned the door handle and slipped inside. She hadn't turned off the light in the adjoining bathroom, so he could see her on top of her bed, curled into a ball at the foot, asleep. Even though she wore a robe and slippers, she looked cold. And cute, like a teenager at a slumber party, in her bright colors.

He debated what to do. Pull the quilt over her where she lay, or tuck her in bed, where she would probably sleep better, all in all. One action probably wouldn't wake her; the other probably would.

James watched her for a little while. She didn't look peaceful. Her expression changed, as if acting out a dream, one filled with events that made her frown. He wished he could stroke her hair, soothe her into a better dream.

Deciding she would be pretty ticked that he was staring at her while she slept, he folded back the bedding as far as he could without folding it on top of her. From the bottom of the bed he lifted her.

"Shh," he said when she jolted awake and held up a fist. "It's just me. You fell asleep on top of the bed."

She relaxed slightly. "Oh."

"You looked cold." He set her down closer to the pillows, then bent to take off her slippers, gave her feet a brief massage. He could feel her staring at the top of his head and wished she would say something. Anything.

"Thank you," she said quietly.

It wasn't what he'd had in mind, he thought with a half smile. He probably should've been more specific in his request. He stood. "See you in the…well, later."

"James, wait." She looked away then back again. "I had been trying to stay awake so I could talk to you." She slipped her hand in her robe pocket and pulled out an envelope. "After I found the letter you sent Paul with your updated address and saw it had been sent to a private mail service, I contacted them. There was one letter in his box that had been there a long time. It was addressed to me, so they released it. Apparently Paul hadn't given them a viable home address and had paid for the box for two years. They'd been trying to figure out what to do with it. Which is a long explanation for what I'm going to show you now. Paul mailed this letter two days before he died."

James sat beside her on the bed. She got up and walked away, keeping her back to him as he opened it and read the single page inside.

Dearest Car,
If you are reading this letter, I am no longer with you. I'm so sorry I made a mess of everything. You shouldn't have to deal with it. I got in too deep. Know that I love you and Kev more than life.
Love always,
Paul

James folded the note, replaced it in the envelope. He didn't wonder why she hadn't shared the letter before. He knew why. "What's your take on it?" James asked Caryn.

"He owed too much, and he couldn't pay. He figured

they were about to do harm. They probably knew he had insurance to cover the debt."

James waited.

"Or," she said, her voice shaking. "He ran away. Couldn't face what he'd done."

James came up behind her, slid his arms around her. Her body shook. After a moment, she turned around and burrowed against him. He stroked her hair, held her tight.

"We can't tell Kevin," she said, her voice strong and sure. "Not unless we find out for sure. He has the right to know the truth—when we know the truth. All right? I don't want him to think his father took the coward's way out."

"Yes." The answer wouldn't change the investigation, nor how they ran it. "So, you've known this for how long?"

"Since the day before I staked out your house."

"Do you think he could've run away?"

"Everything inside me says no. But the letter…"

"Is ambiguous." He leaned back enough to frame her face. "It doesn't change your mind, though, and make you believe as Kevin does, that someone murdered him? If they knew about the insurance, that would be motive enough."

"Either way it's awful. The police say it was an accident. I desperately want to believe that."

"The police didn't have this information. It might make a difference," he said, "depending on what the other facts are—something we won't know until we have all the information."

"I know," she whispered.

"Anything else you're keeping from me?"

She shook her head. "That's it. I promise."

He tucked her close again. "Okay."

"I was too sheltered. Paul took care of everything. That's never going to happen again."

It sounded like a warning, one he didn't need. He understood she was a changed woman from a year ago. Who wouldn't be under the same circumstances? Truth was, he liked this woman. He wasn't too sure he would've wanted someone who deferred to him about everything.

"I should go," he said.

She'd been up on tiptoe. He hadn't realized it until she let her heels touch the floor, taking some of her height away. It swamped him with tenderness, although he didn't know why. He held her hand as they walked to the door. He kissed her lightly, briefly. She threw her arms around him and dragged herself close.

He didn't make even token resistance but hauled her up and kissed her, opening her mouth, finding her tongue, savoring her. He ran his hands down her back, cupped her rear, brought her closer still, aligning their hips, moving against her. She gasped. He kissed her deeper. She groaned. He kissed her harder. She begged wordlessly. He shoved her robe over her shoulders and put his mouth over her breast, the flannel drying his mouth.

He unbuttoned her top and found her flesh, the soft and the hard of her. She arched her back, offering herself, and he dragged his tongue under the soft flesh and over the hard, then he drew her nipple into his mouth, toying with it, teasing her. He felt her hand settle at his waist. She dragged it down him, cupped him, making the pulse there pound rhythmically, potently. He moved her against the wall, slipped a hand inside her pajama bottoms, let his fingers explore the warm wetness of her, eased a finger inside as he lifted his head and watched her face. Her head fell forward. She sank her teeth into his shoulder as her hips moved frantically then went motionless, but still taut and arched forward. Then she moved, steadily, powerfully. He gloried in her response.

She finally slowed, relaxed. He buttoned her pajamas, picked up her robe and tossed it onto the bed.

"What about—"

"Shh," he said, kissing her. "That was risky enough. See you in the morning."

He made his way to his bedroom, yanked off his clothes and stepped into the shower, not cold, but not too hot, either. Her scent mingled with the steam, filling the space. He didn't want to wash it away, but he reached for the soap anyway.

The complications just kept getting deeper.

And so did his feelings.

Thirteen

"I thought it was just gonna be us," Kevin said the next day, his arms crossed. They'd just finished lunch.

Caryn put the leftovers in the refrigerator, letting James deal with Kevin.

"Lyndsey is a CPA. Her husband, Nate Caldwell, is one of the owners of the firm I work for. We need their help, especially Lyndsey's. They're on their way from the airport now."

"Where will they stay?"

"In my room. I'll sleep on the couch."

Kevin tossed his napkin on the counter. "How many more people are you gonna tell about how Dad messed up?"

Caryn met James's gaze. She understood Kevin's hurt, but she knew they both had to swallow their pride if they wanted to resolve everything. How James stayed so cool amazed her, especially when Kevin got visibly angry.

"Do you want answers? Do you want to get back to your life?" James asked.

Kevin nodded, once, rigidly.

"Then this is the fastest way. They won't tell anyone."

"But they'll *know*."

"They know much worse about a lot of people."

"That makes it okay?" Kevin stalked out of the room.

Caryn saw him veer into the living room, so she guessed he was going back to work. It was her first moment alone with James since…last night. He gave her a crooked smile that said more than words.

"So, how are you?" he asked.

"Somewhat…satisfied," she said, flirting. "How about you?"

"Not."

"I offered."

"I hope to take you up on that offer one of these days."

Whew. When he turned his attention to something, he did it all the way. She felt the heat from his eyes from across the counter. "You're very patient with him, James."

"No reason to lose patience. Plus, today… It's hard on both of you."

Caryn hadn't awakened with the anniversary on her mind, but James instead. It hadn't taken long for her to remember, but for a few moments she was just a woman like any other woman, trying to figure out a man, trying to do what was best for her son and herself, trying to move forward in life.

The doorbell rang. Caryn followed James to the door, was introduced to the couple, Lyndsey with her curly brown hair and green glasses that matched her eyes, and Nate with his attractive blond surfer looks. James offered them lunch, which they declined, took them to the office and left them there to work, then he, Caryn and Kevin dived into the rest of the boxes.

Hours went by. Even with music playing in the background, the house seemed extraordinarily quiet, Caryn thought as she watched Kevin and James working side by side, their heads together, examining a stack of papers. How alike they were. And yet different. Some of Paul was in Kevin, too, in a few of his gestures and word inflections. And some of herself, too, she hoped, things she probably never noticed.

Nate wandered in. "Do you have the IOUs, Caryn?"

"Aren't they in there?"

"No."

She looked around the room. "They wouldn't be with these materials. I kept them— Oh. I kept them in one of my cookbooks."

Everyone zeroed in on her. "I figured Kevin would never open one," she said with a shrug. "I was going to rent a safe-deposit box, but I forgot. I'll go get them."

"I will," Kevin said, standing, then hesitating. "Look, my plans tonight were with Emmaline. Can I go there after I get the receipts?"

Caryn looked at James and nodded slightly.

"It's okay with me," he said. "Except you can't drive yourself."

Kevin crossed his arms. "I'm not going to see Venus. That's a promise. I told you we were only friends."

"Someone will come get you in the morning," James said. "Sleep in, if you want, then give us a call. My mother makes the best waffles."

Caryn saw James look outside to evaluate how dark it

was. Dark enough, she decided, when he said to Nate, "Could you take him in my BMW? You can leave and return through the garage that way. Kevin, you need to—"

"Crouch down in the back seat. I know. Same rules as coming."

After Kevin and Nate left the room, James looked at Caryn. "We should be thinking about dinner, I guess. We'll just order in. Got a favorite in mind?"

"I like everything. You might ask Lyndsey, though. Pregnant women sometimes can't tolerate certain foods."

"Pregnant?" He looked in the direction of the office.

Caryn put a hand over her mouth, appalled at herself. "I'm sorry. I just assumed you knew. Oh, shoot."

"How can you tell?"

"I just…can."

"Hmm. I wonder why they haven't said anything. Dana, the wife of Sam Remington, one of the other L.A. partners is pregnant, too. They announced it last week."

"Well, don't bring it up to Nate or Lyndsey. They must have a reason for keeping it to themselves. Just ask what kind of food she and Nate would like."

"Yeah, okay."

Caryn took a moment to stretch her legs. After he went out the doorway she sat in James's overstuffed chair and closed her eyes. It had felt all day like a family day. Her eyes stung at the crazy thought. Their relationship was so new and so strange, yet it felt natural and normal and… right.

"Lyndsey says anything with mashed potatoes," James said, returning.

"Comfort food."

"I know just the place." He left again then just as quickly

returned and walked right up to her. He leaned his hands on the arms of the chair and kissed her, and nothing short and sweet, either, but a kiss that felt distinctly like foreplay. She brought her hands to his face, slipped her thumbs along his lips.

James suddenly turned his head toward the door. Caryn didn't see anything.

"I think we were observed, Mysterious."

"Is that a problem?"

"Not as far as I'm concerned. Lyndsey knows how to keep secrets. I'd better go see what she wanted, though."

Some kiss, Caryn thought. Some amazing kiss.

A while later, the four adults ate a leisurely dinner of Mama Jo's Down Home Comfort Food—chicken and dumplings, mashed potatoes, corn, and banana pudding—while dissecting what Nate and Lyndsey had learned so far.

"My roughest preliminary estimate," Lyndsey said, "is that Paul could have owed the eight hundred thousand dollars that you paid, but I doubt it was actually that much. Any wins would be applied to the debt. Pay up or else." She shrugged at Caryn. "I've handled quite a few cases like this at ARC. I recognize the pattern."

"So, you're making an educated guess," James said.

"That's what it amounts to, yes. I've got more to check, though." She yawned.

"Tomorrow," Nate said, sliding an arm around her shoulder. "You've done enough for today."

James looked at his watch. Not even eight o'clock and Lyndsey was ready for bed. Caryn must be right about the pregnancy. "Yes, tomorrow is fine," James said.

"I'm all right—"

Nate shook his head. He and his wife exchanged a look,

then Nate added, "We're going to spend the night with Sam and Dana, though. I'm sorry we didn't let you know right away. Lyndsey and Dana want to catch up, and I've got some business with Sam. It worked out that they were in San Francisco for the weekend. Plus I'd like him to take a look at the IOUs."

James wasn't about to look a gift horse in the mouth. He and Caryn would have the house to themselves. He didn't offer even token resistance to the plan. He did note, however, that Caryn got awfully busy with clearing the table, never once making eye contact.

Twenty minutes later they were alone in the house.

"They hadn't planned to stay with Sam and Dana," Caryn said, as they stood in the foyer after saying goodbye. "Lyndsey saw us kissing, and decided after Kevin wasn't coming back to give us time alone."

"You think?" He figured as much, too. If he were the one in charge of pay raises, he would be lining Lyndsey up for one right now.

Caryn just stared at him.

He set his hands on her shoulders. "It doesn't mean anything has to happen, Mysterious. When you think about it, we hardly know each other." Yet he felt as though he'd known her for years. Go figure. Now that he stopped to consider it, it probably wasn't such a good idea, after all. "And tonight, of all nights," he added. "Maybe the timing's all wrong."

"We'll see how the evening goes," she said.

"Right."

The evening dragged. They finally had everything sorted. There wasn't a place to step that didn't have a piece of paper on it. It was time to start dumping. Box upon box was filled with never-to-be-needed-again bills and receipts. Warranties for long-ago-tossed appliances and tools were also dumped. A *maybe* box was started. A couple of *keep* boxes, too. At almost midnight Caryn pushed her hands against her lower back and straightened.

"No more," she said.

He nodded. "This is good. There's enough done that Kevin won't wonder how we spent the evening, and enough left for him to help finish up tomorrow."

"We're *good*."

He grinned.

"James, if Lyndsey is right, and Paul didn't owe that much money, what's the next step?"

"Find out who bilked you."

"You can do that?"

"Hope so."

"Do you think it's the same people who were watching you—or me—or whoever it was they were really watching?"

"Maybe."

"You're full of certainty, aren't you?"

"My job is to be right. Being right entails being cautious, so that the wrong people don't get tagged while the right ones get off."

She rubbed her temples. "You're right, of course. I just want it over and done."

He moved close to her and put his arms around her, drawing her near. He pushed the heels of his hands into her lower back. She groaned.

"This is harder than waitressing," she said.

"You're just used to your job. You've used different muscles today." He felt her relax against him, and he widened the area he rubbed, from her shoulders down to her tailbone. "I've got a spa tub."

"You do?"

"You're welcome to use it."

She said nothing.

"Alone," he added, in case that was worrying her. He figured she'd been direct about everything else. She'd be direct about this, too.

"What about after that?"

Her words were muffled by his chest, but he heard them. "Up to you, Caryn."

"You're not going to just take charge and let me off the hook?"

He wanted to. He'd rather they just be swept away, unable to stop themselves. But they were mature, responsible adults, capable of making rational decisions about sex. Ten years ago, hell, *five* years ago, he might have done as she said. But there was too much riding on this relationship not to think it through. They had a lifetime of contact ahead. As she said once, they would even be grandparents together.

Which was also why they needed to sleep together and get it over with now, before they made too much of it, before they made it too important. Do it now. End the curiosity. Become friends instead of lovers. Easy.

"I think I'll take you up on your offer," she said.

Which one?

"Any tricks to using the tub?" she asked.

"Fill the tub to a couple inches above the jets, then push the big chrome button. It'll stay on for ten minutes at a time."

She stepped away from him. "Where will you be?"

"Down here until I hear you head to your room."

"Okay. Thanks." She patted his cheek and left.

Bemused, he watched her go. Everyone had set them up for a night of unbridled, uninhibited, uninterrupted sex.

And she was going to sleep.

The phone rang. It was the police, and, for once, it was good news.

Fourteen

Caryn couldn't understand how she could come out of a long, relaxing soak amid a profusion of soothing, bubbling jets and be more tense than when she stepped in. She should have been as loose as overcooked spaghetti, and sleepwalking to her guest room by now. Instead she was wound up, fired up and heated up—for James.

If she'd brought a beautiful nightgown with her, it would be an easier decision. She wanted to look incredible for him. She wanted her armor —her perfume and lotions that sat on her dresser at home. She wanted the pink lightbulb she had in her little lamp on her bedside table. She was forty-one years old. She'd slept with one man her entire life, and he'd been dead a year. And she was lonely and…horny. She smiled at the word, which seemed better suited for a man, but she couldn't think of another word that fit her situation better.

Instead she sat on the edge of his tub with a fluffy blue towel wrapped around her, staring at her flannel pajamas jumbled on the vanity counter. They hadn't been a turnoff to James last night. He'd kissed her while she wore them. Unbuttoned the top. Put his mouth on her breasts. Slid his hand...

She stood, looked at herself in the mirror. Her face had a glow she hadn't seen in a very long time—probably from the hot water, but who cared? It made her look young and lively. Her hair was damp at the ends. She fluffed it then let it fall where it may. Definitely a tousled, sexy look. Lipstick? Yes. Only because it was the kind that couldn't be kissed off.

A bit of mascara and she was done. She was ready—if her answer was yes.

She stared at the floor for at least a minute then looked toward the ceiling. "I think you would want me to be happy," she whispered. "I think this would make me happy. For now. I know the future isn't in our cards. But for tonight? What's the harm?"

She nodded her head, then padded across his thick carpet to the bedroom door. She pulled it open, closed it with one sonic-boom short of a slam, making sure he could hear it. Then she walked to his bed, pulled back the bedding, climbed on top and knelt in the middle of it, holding tight to her towel with both hands.

She waited. And waited. And waited. Her legs started to tingle and ache. She fidgeted, wiggled her toes, straightened her legs, rotated her ankles. Still no James.

Her instep cramped just as she was about to climb off the bed and go in search of him. The door opened, catching her with one leg on the bed and one on the floor, the towel slipping from above and spreading open from below.

The cramp tightened, curling her toes. Great. Just great. She'd gone from sexy lady to pained contortionist in two seconds flat.

"Ow," she said, unable to stop herself. She started walking and the cramp tightened even more.

"What's wrong?"

"I have a cramp in my foot," she muttered, embarrassed.

He came forward. "I heard the door…I thought you'd gone to your room," he said, looking confused.

Good. If she was going to look ridiculous, the least he could do was look confused.

"I didn't leave," she said.

"I used all my investigative skills to conclude that myself." He moved her back to sit on the bed, picked up her foot and pushed his thumb into her instep.

She almost screamed, then it eased. He worked at it for at least a minute in silence.

"Is this a yes, Caryn?" he asked quietly.

"Yes." The word jammed in her throat, but her lips shaped the letters. She tried again. "What took you so long?"

"I was trying to get over my disappointment before I came to bed. If I'd known you were waiting…" He kept her feet in his lap, his hands resting on her shins. "We've wasted ten minutes."

"Fifteen. But who's counting?"

His hair was damp. He must have taken a shower somewhere else in the house.

"Are you sure?" he asked. "You know what I mean… about tonight being the night?"

"It's past midnight. That day is over." *And a new life begins.*

"You are beautiful."

The reverence in his voice flipped a switch inside her. Whatever doubts, whatever concerns she had, disappeared in that instant.

"I'll be right back," he said, moving her legs aside. He went to his fireplace and lit it. A moment later, he turned a dial next to the door, and music filled the room, soft and bluesy. He turned off the lights, letting the flames of the gaslit fire provide the ambience.

Then he walked back to the bed.

She opened her arms to him. The towel almost fell, but didn't. She watched him take off his shoes, socks and T-shirt then he moved into her embrace and held her, just held her. She inhaled the scent of him, soapy and clean. Her cheek rested against his chest until he tipped her head back and kissed her.

She thought she knew how he kissed, but she'd only had a sample, an appetizer. This was the main course—possession. Beneath a surface taste of toothpaste was heat and desire and need, flavors so rare and coveted that she felt privileged just to be offered a morsel. He didn't scrimp on the quantities, either, but offered heaping servings of everything, letting her know how hungry he was for her, too. She savored every glide of his tongue, every nibble of his teeth, every brush of his lips. His hands dived into her hair, his large palms and long fingers cupping her head, making her feel safe and protected and…wanted. Were those sounds coming from her? She didn't care. She just wanted to feel…him, every part of him.

He moved off the bed and stripped off his jeans, and there he was, in all his beautiful glory. For me, she thought. All for me. She couldn't wait to get her hands on him. She reached for him.

His expression fierce, he hooked a hand in her towel and tugged. The cloth fell to the bed. He balled it up and heaved it aside. She felt twenty again, and virginal, except this time she knew what the possibilities could be.

"I need to touch you," she said.

"I need you to touch me."

She grabbed his hands and guided him to lie down. She felt his eyes roving over her, and she was aware of how hard her nipples were, how her breasts moved as she did, how wet she was. But, oh, she didn't want to rush. He would be a lifetime memory, she knew that with all her heart, which was beating harder every minute and feeling more vulnerable by the second. She didn't need the complication of falling in love, but it seemed to be happening, beyond her control.

Stopping the internal debate, she placed her hands on his head, combed his hair with her fingers, enjoying the soft fullness. She dragged her hands down his face, stroking his forehead, brushing her fingertips over his eyebrows then his eyelids, then his cheeks, his nose, his lips, his chin. He'd shaved. His cheeks and jaw felt smooth. She bent to run her tongue along his jaw, lightly over his lips, then down his neck. She let a hand drift down him, then sat up again so she could watch, aware of his eyes, open and watching her in return.

She found a distinct scar on his left shoulder, slid her fingertips over it. "Is this where you were shot?"

"Yeah."

"Did it hurt?"

"Like hell."

She traced another scar on the other side, and one lower, closer to his stomach. "What about these?"

"Knives."

She cringed. "Maybe you should find a different occupation?"

"I did. And I'm not planning to get any more scars."

"Are there more than these?"

"A couple. Big one on my back from a piece of metal when I was shoved once. One on the front…lower."

She let herself look all down him and saw a jagged scar.

"I was lucky," he said. "An inch to the right…"

She kissed the spot, followed the uneven line with her tongue as he sucked in a breath and arched off the bed. His hand came down hard on her wrist, and he pulled her up and away, bringing her down beside him, her face close to his.

"You don't know what you're doing to me," he rasped.

Flattered and thrilled she smiled leisurely. "I'm not done."

"Yeah, you are. For now, you are."

"I don't think so." She reached down to wrap him in her hand, felt his body go rigid with resistance, fighting off what her efforts were doing to him. Curious, she stroked him, swirled a fingertip over the very top of him, catching a drop of fluid, and spreading it—

He sat up, flattened her on her back and tortured her, getting even in the best possible way. She gave up control and let herself just feel. Sensation bombarded her, building and ebbing, building again, higher. His hands were everywhere, then his mouth followed. She shook, then at some point she begged.

He moved over her, nudging her legs open, finding his place. Home. "Open your eyes," he said, an order, but a quiet one.

She saw the need in his eyes, too, that he'd reached the point of no return along with her. She raised her knees. He laid his fingers where everything throbbed, stroked her, separated her, then he angled his body so that he could slip inside her, going slowly, letting her feel herself open up to him. She couldn't stop the orgasm that slammed into her before he was embedded, nor the next one that happened the moment he was all the way inside, nor the third one that came fast on the heels of the others when he moved rhythmically inside her. He didn't hold back, either, and his pleasure seemed to last a long time before he finally draped himself over her, both of them dragging in air. She was a little in shock at the intensity of what had happened. In shock, in awe, in utter glory and gratitude.

After a minute, he rolled to his side, taking her with him, wrapping her close and tight.

"Damn," he said.

"My thought exactly." She smiled against his chest.

"I need to get up for a second."

She pulled back to let him out. He'd put on protection before the critical moment, and she was grateful. She hadn't even thought about it, hadn't ever had to worry about birth control. Wouldn't that have been a mess if she'd gotten pregnant?

He slipped back into bed and she went right back into his arms. It felt so good to be held, to feel his body next to hers, to smell him and touch him and—

"A twenty-percent tip for your thoughts, Mysterious."

"I'm just happy." She snuggled a little closer. "I feel like I've been given the best present ever."

"Me, too."

She wasn't sure how true that could be. He must have had more than his share of relationships through the years. How could this one be any better than any other? But she wasn't about to question him, not while they were naked and warm and satisfied.

The fire burned, the music played, but time didn't stop. It was after 2:00 a.m. Morning would be here soon enough. Kevin would be back. Lyndsey and Nate. How was she going to get through the day without touching James? Without smiling at him? Without being reminded every second that they'd made love. What kind of acting skill was that going to take?

"You're worried about tomorrow," he said.

She tipped her back to look at him. "How'd you know that?"

"You stiffened up. Don't worry about it, okay? Unless Kevin is specifically looking for something between us, he won't notice. He won't know that Nate and Lyndsey didn't spend the night. They'll be here before him."

"Are you sure?"

"He's a teenager. He'll sleep in, then he'll want breakfast. I don't expect him before ten at the earliest. The thing is, we can't go out of our way to avoid each other, either. That's when he would catch on."

"I suppose you're right." She settled against him again.

"Want some good news? The police got a print on Baldy. He's a known low-level crook. Never carries a gun. He's in jail."

Whatever little amount of steam she'd had left in her, dissipated. "We're safe?"

"From him, certainly. But the fact he wasn't carrying also tells us something. He was probably not here to do anything other than watch and report."

He stroked her hair. She closed her eyes, enjoying being pampered and cherished.

"Sleep," he said, softly, tenderly.

She had expected it would be strange to sleep with him, with a man she'd known less than two weeks. But she relaxed against him, felt him kiss her forehead and let herself drift off, leaving every worry, every fear behind.

Tomorrow would come soon enough.

Fifteen

"**I** would say that these—" the man held up a handful of IOUs, signed by Paul and countersigned by someone named Johnson "—are signed by Paul Brenley. The rest are forged."

James's mantel clock had just struck noon. Everyone stood huddled around the handwriting expert that Sam Remington, one of the ARC owners, had called in on Lyndsey's advice and his own speculation. The man set all the papers on the coffee table and sat back. James looked at Caryn first, then Kevin. Their expressions were bleak.

Sam, Nate and Lyndsey said nothing.

"How much was the actual amount he owed?" Caryn asked.

"Three hundred and fifty thousand—or so," Lyndsey said.

"So they bilked me out of four hundred and fifty—or so." She transformed, fury mixed with embarrassment replaced shock and despair. "I want my money back."

The investigators exchanged glances. Nate said, "Your chances—"

"I want my money back."

"Jamey," Nate said. "Lyndsey and I are going back to Sam and Dana's. Give us a call when you decide what you want to do."

Within a minute everyone was gone except James, Caryn and Kevin.

"They are not going to get away with this," Caryn said, her voice shaking. "They're not."

Kevin was being extraordinarily quiet. James wondered what he was thinking.

"I'll fix us some lunch if you show me where the stuff is," Kevin said to James.

Surprised, James looked at him. As if Kevin didn't know what was in the refrigerator and where he kept the bread and chips? Then Kevin intensified his stare and angled his head ever so slightly toward the kitchen. James followed him.

"We'll be back in a minute," he said to Caryn as he passed her, touching her briefly on the shoulders and finding her as yielding as concrete.

In the kitchen Kevin shoved his hands through his hair. "Look, man, maybe this is nothin'." He paced a bit, looked back toward the living room, and lowered his voice. "Johnson is a common name."

"Yeah." James ducked his head to hear the boy. "So?"

"So those notes are all signed *Johnson*. Venus's last name is Johnson."

James frowned. "You can't think she could have anything to do with this?"

Kevin's gaze might have turned James into petrified human. "After I told her you were a P.I. she got, you know, chummier with me, was all nervous. Asked more questions. I know it seems crazy, but I keep hearing about how people should trust their instincts. My instincts say there's a connection."

James sorted the idea with what he knew of the girl. She'd been hired shortly after Caryn, had no waitressing experience, had never gotten good at her job, had made friends right away with Caryn and Kevin, although keeping her distance from the boy—until she found out that Caryn's friend was a P.I. Plus she'd turned the heat up on Kevin.

"You could be on to something," James said.

"I know Mom wants the money back. I want that, too— it's a lot—but I want the men who killed my father more."

"That's not a given—that he was killed. Let's take it one step at a time." James needed to see the site where Paul died, talk to the CHP officer who wrote the report. "Who do you think is following us—or me, or whichever of us they're following?"

"Someone who doesn't want us to find out the truth."

"What's the next step?" James asked.

Kevin thought it over. "Talk to Venus."

"Right. Let's go tell your mom what's going on." James started to leave.

Kevin grabbed his arm, stopping him, then looked him in the eye. "You know we're not a family."

"Who?"

"My mom, me and you."

James couldn't find words to reply. He wasn't sure what Kevin was saying, nor was he sure he wanted to know.

"This is too weird, you know, man? I mean, like, I could never introduce you to my friends. People would figure it out by lookin' at us."

"Why are you bringing this up?"

"'Cause my mom and *you*." A flush spread across his face. "You like each other. Do us a favor, okay? When this is over, just go away. I don't want her hurt ever again."

And stay away from you, too? he wanted to ask.

But this was not the time for debates or promises. "We'll worry about all that later," James said. "For now, why don't you give Venus a call and see if she can meet you for lunch, someplace public so I can see if she's being followed or if we are. Someplace no one will have staked out." His mother's house, James decided, where he could leave Kevin, if he had to, knowing he was taken care of. Kevin wouldn't defy Emmaline. "Do you want to be the one to tell your mom what you figured out?" James asked Kevin.

"Can I?"

"It's your discovery."

Kevin grinned. James wanted to wrap his arm around him and pull him close. What a warrior he had turned out to be. He would lay down his life for his mother, that was certain.

And James was an unwanted outsider to him. That was certain, too.

Caryn didn't know who she was more nervous about seeing—Venus or James's mother, Emmaline. If what Kevin and James thought about Venus was true, Caryn had just been dealt another blow, been victim of another deception. That was hard to take.

As for Emmaline, Kevin adored her already. But why shouldn't he? He'd never known Paul's mother, who had died before Kevin was born, and Caryn's mother moved to Arizona a few years ago and rarely saw them. Emmaline was his grandmother, even if in a roundabout way, and she lived in town, and apparently she was a great cook and advice-giver. Caryn would be jealous—if she didn't want it all so much for Kevin.

He had picked up Venus and driven her to a nearby restaurant. When no one appeared to be following any of them, they piled into one car and drove to Emmaline's, Venus asking questions, no one giving any but the vaguest of answers—until they were safely inside the house.

Emmaline hugged Caryn, but out of deference to Venus's presence, no one talked about the relationship. Emmaline went into the kitchen under the guise of preparing a snack, but merely leaving them alone.

Venus's normally rosy-cheeked innocence seemed suddenly faded and guilty. She twisted her fingers together, tried to smile, looked from face-to-face.

"We know about your father," Kevin said.

Caryn felt James react to the statement. She gathered it wasn't the interrogation route he would've taken, but he didn't interrupt, either.

"You know what about my father?"

Kevin leaned toward her. "Do you think I'm stupid? A girl like you isn't interested in a guy like me. You wanted something. It just took me a little while to figure out."

"I don't have a clue what you're talking about. What would I want?"

Kevin didn't answer. He had apparently backed himself in a corner. He looked at James.

"You were sent to spy on Caryn and Kevin," James said.

"Why would I do that?" Her chin went up, her blond curls bounced.

"Because someone needed to keep an eye on them. To see what they were up to."

"Because my father was murdered," Kevin said.

Venus spun toward Kevin. "No!"

"And it was your father who did it," he added.

Color leeched from her face. "My father died ten years ago. And that's the truth."

Silence crash-landed in the room. They were wrong. How could they be wrong? Caryn thought.

"May I speak to you alone?" Venus asked James.

Caryn bristled. She'd trusted this young woman, had enjoyed her company, had taken her in, treated her almost like a daughter. "What you have to say, you say to all of us."

Venus looked at each of them individually, then at the floor. Finally she pushed her hair back from her face. "It's my brother you want. I...I don't know what his business is exactly—" she glared at Kevin "—but it isn't murder."

"He was the one who sent you to keep an eye on Caryn and Kevin," James said.

After a few seconds she nodded.

"He lined up the job at GGC."

"Yes."

"Why did you do it?"

Her eyes filled with tears. She looked away, her hands clenched in her lap, her back stiff. "He was holding something over me. I'm not telling you what. It wasn't criminal or anything, just family stuff. He said if I did this for him, he would let me off the hook."

"We trusted you," Caryn said.

"I know. I'm so sorry." She almost pleaded with her eyes.

"Okay, I've had enough of this. What's next?" Caryn

asked James. Tired of everything happening around her, she was ready to take action.

Plans were made. For now, everyone would go about their lives as before, especially since no one seemed to be under surveillance anymore.

But in a couple of hours James would fly to L.A. with Nate and Sam to investigate Paul's death and determine the cause, armed with the knowledge the CHP didn't have at the time, that there was a possibility Paul was murdered. James shared Paul's note with Nate and Sam, indicating the possibility that he could have been running away, too.

Kevin was furious at James at being left behind. James understood his anger but didn't back down. Kevin made his case, arguing that they wouldn't have figured out what they had so far without him putting two and two together. He may be right, but it didn't change James's mind about how the investigation needed to be handled.

Kevin stayed with Emmaline, although James considered Kevin's reason might be more to irritate James than to promote his relationship with Emmaline. Kevin seemed aware that James envied their bond. He didn't care about the reason. He only wanted the boy safe.

James drove Caryn home and followed her up her stairs, carrying the sacks she'd brought to his house. His gaze on her hips, he remembered how beautiful she was last night, stretched out naked on his bed, flames from the fire like a flickering golden spotlight on her pale skin. She wore a green skirt and white button-up blouse, and her comfortable shoes. He knew her bra was white and lacy. Every so often he would see hints of lace if she leaned a certain way. He remembered a moment from last night where she'd stretched like a cat in a flood of sunshine. How graceful she was. How incredibly sexy. Any hesitation had been tossed away with the towel last night. She'd been open and provocative and demanding, especially in the morning when she'd awakened him with exploring fingers and increasingly hot kisses.

And Kevin wanted him to give her up.

"House is cold," she said, stopping in front of the thermostat and adjusting it.

Kevin wants me to give you up.

He couldn't tell her that. Couldn't even hint at it.

"Do you have to leave right away?" she asked.

"Yeah." He set down her sacks and watched her keep herself busy by straightening pillows that didn't need straightening, and stacking magazines that were barely out of alignment. "Caryn?"

"Hmm?"

He identified her mood. She was trying to seem as if she was okay with everything, when everything had suddenly changed. She'd already been through enough in the past year, but maybe he would give her some answers about Paul, get her money back and help her get started on her new life again.

"I'm going to do everything I possibly can for you," he said.

Kevin wants me to give you up.

"Are you?"

Hold on. What's this? He examined her face. She wasn't trying to come to terms with the newest events. She was ticked off.

"Of course I am," he said.

"I want to go with you," she said, crossing her arms.

"No."

"Yes. It's my life, my problems. I need to be part of the solution."

"This trip is only to talk to the CHP. I'm not doing anything else yet. Johnson is not going anywhere. There's no reason to rush. And I can't do my job well if I have to worry about you, too."

"You're just like him. Like Paul. You take all these stupid risks."

He didn't like being compared to Paul, who, in James's eyes, was weak. He hadn't taken care of his family. "I take *calculated* risks," he said coolly.

"You have scars! I saw then. Touched them."

"I'm alive."

She made a sound of frustration, as if she couldn't get her point across, then she went up on tiptoe and kissed him. He resisted for a second, maybe two before pulling her close and devouring her mouth, taking everything she gave, giving back even more.

"I'm afraid you're going to get hurt," she whispered. "I'm so afraid. Then who will...Kevin have?"

He heard her hesitation but ignored it. He couldn't encourage her, either, not with Kevin's demand weighing on him. Maybe Paul hadn't done his job, but James would. He would make sure his son—yes, *his son*—would have his answers and his future secure.

"I have to go," he said, holding her arms and moving her back.

"Already?"

He had a little time, but he didn't think it would make a difference. There was only so much that could be said.

She put her hands on his face. "Make love with me again. Please."

Unpredictable. She'd gone from being angry to—
She began unbuttoning his shirt. "Don't leave yet."

"I don't have much time."

"I don't think it's going to take long, Jamey."

Jamey. It was the first time she'd called him that. He swooped down, tipping her head back, kissing her like it was the last time, which it may be for them—if Kevin got his way. James didn't want to think about that. He just wanted to feel…her, every curve, every plane, every soft and hard place on her body. He wanted to kiss her until he couldn't breathe, hold her until his arms shook, love her until she screamed.

He stripped her where they stood, finding the white lacy bra and panties he'd known he would find, then removing them, neither gently nor slowly. He peeled off his own clothes, lifted her so that her legs straddled his hips and then carried her to her bedroom.

Feminine, just like her, he thought, aware of the room. A cream-colored bedspread and pillows with lacy edges. He dropped her in the middle of the bed and came down on her, merging mouths that were on fire with need and expectation. He stayed there attacking her mouth until she breathed as though she'd run a marathon. He moved down her body, drew one hard nipple into his mouth, then the other. His tongue swirled and teased. His lips measured and pulled. His teeth scraped. He filled his hands with the soft flesh surrounding the hard peaks.

After a while he pushed himself lower; she lifted her hips higher. He tasted her, cherished her, then slowed down, gentled his actions, taking his time. Her hands pushed against his head; she grasped his hair. She rocked, arched. Enjoyed. He lunged over her, plunged into her, felt her hot, tight welcome. Was surrounded by it. Didn't want to give it up. But his body had other ideas, other needs.

She pulled his head down for a kiss, openmouthed, demanding, without tenderness, with unchecked passion. Without caution, with urgency. They hit the pinnacle together, and there was something in the mutuality that shot him higher, made it last longer.

He kissed her, a long, lingering kiss meant to soften the impact. She looked as serious as she had before they'd fallen into bed.

"Do you promise you won't do anything yet?"

No, he couldn't promise. Things could happen. He didn't know, couldn't predict for sure. "I can't promise, Caryn. I've told you what the plan is. And you can't take time off from work, anyway. You've already told me you could lose your job if you don't show up."

"Do you know how many restaurants are in this city? Three thousand. Think I can't get another job?"

"One as good?"

"One better." She shifted.

"I understand Kevin being mad at me, but not you. You should be seeing the big picture."

She sighed. "I can call you?"

"As often as you like."

"Don't be mad," she said with a smile.

"I'm not mad." He wanted to tell her how beautiful she was, but it would only complicate things when they returned and he had to let her go.

As if just having sex with her wouldn't complicate—

He hadn't used birth control. None. Hadn't even considered it. Neither had she said anything. What were they thinking? They could not, at their ages, find themselves pregnant. Kevin already couldn't deal with explaining James. What about if they had a baby together?

Well, there was nothing he could do about it now. He had to wait, like a teenager after prom night had gotten out of hand.

Except…why did the idea make him start imagining a family again, but this time, people with faces he could put to them. And personalities.

The image took root, and held. He kissed her goodbye but didn't linger. Fate would do what it would do.

Sixteen

"**I** owe you for this," James said to Nate and Sam as they waited in an interview room for the highway patrol officer who'd investigated Paul's accident. "You've got other jobs to do." Hell, they were two of the owners of the ARC. Partners. He was just an investigator on staff.

"First," Sam said, "we look after our own. Second, it's kind of entertaining watching you fall head over heels." He glanced at Nate. "We've both been there and done that. I don't know about Nate, but I didn't realize how stupid I got while I was falling in love with Dana. You need someone at your back, because you won't be thinking straight."

Nate laughed quietly. "Amen, brother."

James might have opened up and talked about his concerns to Cassie, but these were the power guys. He couldn't tell them how tenuous his relationship with Caryn was, or the reason behind it. They would…scoff? Advise him to just do what he wanted to do, that Kevin would come around eventually? He didn't want that. He wanted Kevin to come around first, he thought, as Sergeant Hal Bodine walked in and set a folder on the table in front of James. He remained standing. Pushing fifty, James decided, and in top physical form.

"I remember everything about this one," Bodine said. "I only brought the file to show you the photos. The kid, the son of the victim, kept coming in and cornering me to keep looking for different answers."

James dragged the open file close, angling it so that Sam and Nate could see it, too. They flipped through the photos. He winced. "Kevin, the son, he didn't see these, did he?"

Bodine stared at James. "No."

They read and talked about the report—how it had been raining, how a cement truck had dumped a load the day before right on that curve. "I figured Brenley started into a slide and never righted it. There was still some gravel and sand on the road from the cement truck. It was wet."

"Could it have been hit-and-run?" Sam asked.

Bodine gave an exhausted sigh, as if giving a stock speech he'd given a dozen times before. "There's not as much evidence with bikes as with cars. But we can still put facts together. The majority of the damage was on the left side of the bike, as you can see. He slipped and never recovered, went over the embankment."

"Did you *look* for hit-and-run?" James asked.

"I *looked* for everything."

"I wasn't insulting you, Sergeant," James said. "I need to lay this to rest for the son."

"The kid came to see me, five maybe six times. What am I supposed to tell him? He says how his father knows that road, every inch of it. That he's a careful man. Well, I know that road, too, and I've almost lost it on that curve myself a few times. There is no evidence to indicate foul play. It could've been a hit-and-run, intentional or otherwise, but I don't think so. I found absolutely nothing to indicate otherwise."

"Does anything indicate he applied the brakes?" James asked.

Bodine raised his brows. "Are you saying this could be self-inflicted? Intentional on Brenley's part?"

"I'm asking, not saying."

The sergeant scratched his cheek, then he flipped through the photos until he came to the one he wanted. "No skid marks, but the road was wet," he reminded them. "And personally if I was gonna take my last ride, it wouldn't be here. It'd be a mile up the road. If Brenley knew the road as good as the kid said he did, he'd know that, too."

James nodded.

"Do you think the boy will rest now?" Bodine asked. "I've got a kid about that age. I kept wanting to hug him. He was struggling for answers."

"I'll do my best to convince him," James said, standing and extending his hand. "Thanks a lot."

"What next?" Sam asked when they left the building.

He thought about Caryn, who was going about her life, being patient, he hoped. And he thought about Kevin, probably still ticked off—as if he needed more fuel to dislike James. And he thought about Venus, whom he'd decided was as much a victim as Caryn and Kevin.

What next?

He didn't have a doubt in his mind.

* * *

James got the last flight back to San Francisco that night, the longest Sunday of his life. He should just go home, fall into bed, and sleep until he'd had enough, even if he didn't get up until noon. He couldn't see Caryn and Kevin until after three o'clock, anyway.

He glanced at his dashboard clock as he pulled onto Highway 101, leaving the airport. Almost midnight. He wanted to see Caryn, talk to her, tell her what they decided to do. He could've told her over the phone, but he needed to tell her in person, because *he* needed to be with her.

His cell phone rang, and he knew it was her without even looking at the screen. "Mysterious."

A pause, then, "How'd you guess it was me?"

"Just lucky." Her voice flowed through him like liquid fire. Even though he'd been sure nothing would happen while he was gone, a part of him worried anyway, as a man does about a woman he…loves. His heart slammed against his sternum. "How are you?"

"Fine. Not sleepy, though. Could you come over?"

"Kevin—"

"Went to sleep a couple of hours ago. He sleeps like the dead. I just…I just want to talk. I can't wait until tomorrow."

And he wanted to hold her, kiss her, sleep beside her. That's all. Just sleep. He didn't have that right. Would never have that right.

"Please," she added.

He should take his moments while he could, he supposed. What difference would it make in the long run? "Okay. I'm about twenty minutes out."

"I'll be watching for you. You won't have to knock."

"See you soon," he said, knowing he was just opening

himself up to heartache, but also knowing he couldn't live his life any other way. His son and his son's mother would come first. Now and always.

"What can I get you?" Caryn asked after James eased out a kitchen chair and sat at the table. "Have you had dinner?"

"Hamburger at the airport. What I'd really like is hot chocolate."

"Comfort food?" she asked, studying him. He hadn't attempted to hug her since he'd arrived. She was so tired of waiting to hear what happened. He'd put her off twice during the day, with flimsy excuses. No more excuses now.

"It's been a long day," he said.

She grabbed milk and a pan, then the box of powdered cocoa. No microwaved stuff, no watered-down cocoa, but the old-fashioned kind. Besides it gave her something to do—stir the milk so it wouldn't scorch, keep herself busy. She kept her back to him, waiting for him to set the pace and give her the facts, but her pulse thundered with expectation. *Tell me, tell me, tell me.*

"It was an accident, Caryn."

She dropped the spoon to the floor, pressed her hands to her mouth. "Are you sure?"

"Positive."

She hadn't heard him move, but he was there, behind her. She turned and fell into him. His arms came around her and tightened, in comfort and sympathy and celebration of an agony shattered. She could pick up the pieces and put them back together in a new arrangement, a happier one. She had James to thank for that.

He tucked her face against his neck. She hadn't known how much it had weighed on her until the weight was lifted. Everything let loose at once—the anger and shame, gone. Grief transitioned into a gentler emotion with good memories attached instead of the horrible ones. She could remember Paul with love now.

After a while she stepped back and grabbed a tissue. James picked up the spoon from the floor, got another one out of a drawer and stirred. She leaned over and sniffed the concoction. It didn't seem to have scorched. "Where do we go from here?" She gave her cheeks one more swipe with the tissue and tucked it in her pocket.

"You want to hear my plan?"

The twinkle in his eye alerted her that she was about to be fed a line.

"I figure we need to close this out now, before anything else happens. How about a plan to have Venus tell her brother that she's turning state's evidence." His look was mock serious. "He'll come rushing up from L.A., intending to take her home, get her out of sight. But I'll be hiding out at her place, instead, and *grab* him. Then I'll hold him hostage for the five hundred grand—that's counting interest—he owes you. When he's turned over the money, he'll be free to go."

She grinned at the ridiculousness of his idea, grateful he'd chosen to change the mood so drastically. He always seemed attuned to her needs.

"You won't give him the option of turning himself in?"

"To the police?"

"No, to the tooth fairy."

He managed not to smile. "Somehow I don't see him turning himself in. Better to take him down and do it myself."

"You're not calling in the cops?"

"They'd just mess things up. They always do on TV."

"Can I help?"

"I don't see why not." He turned the heat off from under the pan. "Got a couple of mugs?"

She pulled two from the cupboard and set them down.

"What was that?" James asked suddenly, turning toward the kitchen door.

"What?"

"That sound."

"Um, I just put the mugs on the counter."

"No." He abandoned the pan and walked into the living room, then over to the stairs.

She followed. "I didn't hear anything." After a minute they returned to the kitchen and sat at the table, opposite each other. The cocoa was warm and sweet. Her cares were lifted. Life was good, she thought. "So, what's the *real* plan?" she asked.

"You didn't like that one?" he asked, with the same twinkle.

"Well, I hope you're going to let the legal system do their job." If James was contemplating even for a moment the idea of going after Johnson, she'd find a way to kidnap him herself, just to keep James safe.

"Why do you hope that?"

"Because I believe in the system."

"Even though you didn't contact the police yourself about the extortion?"

"Because I didn't. I learned. We've got enough evidence, right?"

"Maybe. Depends on his lawyers. I have to be honest, you may not see the money. Even if he's convicted, he probably won't pay up. It's hard to say."

"I have everything I need, Jamey."

He cocked his head at her. "That's a change from this morning, when you said you wanted your money back."

"I've had time to think, and to get my priorities back in alignment. Sure it would be wonderful to have the money, but it's not what counts the most."

"What does count?"

"Home, family, good food, friends, world peace." She smiled.

"You are one of a kind." He leaned across the table and kissed her, her mouth warm and chocolatey.

"I need to go to bed," he said. "I'll call Kevin before he heads to school and set up a time to meet with both of you around three-thirty. Unless you want me to talk to him alone."

"Would you be telling him anything you haven't told me?"

"No."

"Then feel free to talk to him early in the morning. I'm sure he'll be calling you if you don't call him, anyway."

He took her hand and walked with her to the top of stairs. "Don't come down with me," he said.

"I have to. I need to turn the dead bolt after you go."

At the bottom of the stairs she waited for a kiss. Instead he cupped her face with one hand, brushed his thumb along her cheek, then left.

She locked the door and leaned against it. She didn't know how long it would take before Johnson could be arrested. Days, maybe. Weeks, even. A case would have to be built. They would have to live in limbo until then, but at least some of her questions were answered.

And now there was a big one ahead. What will happen between her and James? She couldn't begin to guess. All she knew for sure was that, as crazy as it seemed, she'd fallen in love with him.

Seventeen

The ringing phone dragged James from a deep, dreamless sleep. He grabbed it on the second ring, glancing at the clock at the same time. Five minutes before six.

"Venus called in sick."

He threw his legs over the side of the bed. "When?"

"Just now." Caryn's voice was hushed, as if afraid she might be overheard.

"Did you talk to her?"

"No. Raphael did."

"What'd she say was wrong?"

"He didn't pass that along."

"Okay. I'll try to get in touch with her. Don't worry, okay? She's probably reacting to everything that's happened."

"Sure. Can I call you later?"

"Of course."

He hung up, found Venus's number and dialed it. An answering machine picked up. "Venus, it's James. Are you there?… Pick up, please." He waited a while longer before setting down the receiver. He didn't like his gut feeling.

He yanked on some clothes and headed downstairs, deciding to go see her, even though her apartment was a half hour away in clear traffic.

It wasn't clear traffic today. He drummed his fingers on the steering wheel, took a few side streets. He planned ahead for the day. After he talked with Kevin later, he would go to the office and work out the details with Cassie and Quinn, probably include Nate and Sam by conference call. Next step would be notifying the D.A. of Johnson's county, and while James would leave the job in their hands, he wouldn't back out altogether. For himself, as well as Caryn and Kevin, he would stay involved. He'd figured out how to have good working relationships with the police and district attorneys through his career. They might not encourage outside participation in an investigation, but they always appreciated good evidence.

He was almost at Venus's apartment when his phone rang.

"Paladin."

"It's Kevin."

"Hi. I was going to call you later—"

"Um, I think we're kinda in trouble." His words were rushed, his voice low.

"We?"

"Venus and me."

"Where are you?"

"In my apartment."

Make a U-turn, head east.

"We just came from Venus's place, when we realized what we'd done was kinda…" The words faded.

"What are you doing there?" The traffic jammed again. *C'mon. C'mon.*

"I was waiting last night for you. I sorta heard you talkin' to Mom about, you know, your plan to trap Johnson—"

Every curse James had learned in his life echoed in his head. That stupid scenario he'd created for Caryn. That damned stupid scenario. "What'd you do?" He passed a car on the right. A horn blared.

"I went to see Venus right away. We decided to just do it, you know? Take care of business, like you planned. But—" his voice dropped "—I'm a little scared now. I don't even have a gun. We've been stupid, I think. Can you—"

"I'm on my way, Kev. Now listen to me. You and Venus get out of there. He knows where you live, too. Are you on your cell phone?"

"Yeah."

"Okay. Just hold on a minute. Don't move until I tell you to."

"Okay."

The fear in his voice shook James to the core. "It's going to be all right. Hang on."

He put Kevin on hold long enough to call the police and have a unit sent out, then he clicked back in. "Okay, Kev, just keep talking to me. You and Venus leave the apartment right now. Get in your car and just drive."

"Where to?"

"It doesn't matter. Just drive."

"Okay. Venus, come on…. Okay, we're leaving."

James heard Venus scream, not long and loud but enough to show fear. A door slammed.

"What's going on, Kev?"

"He's here! Johnson!"

"Did he see you?"

"I don't know."

"Go out your back door and upstairs to your mom's. Get into a closet and stay quiet. Do not do anything—do you understand me?"

"Yeah. I'm sorry…."

"Just *go*. Keep your phone on. I'm two minutes away." James kept his phone propped between his shoulder and ear as he navigated the last few blocks. It seemed like an hour—

"He's breaking in, man! He came up the back and knocked out the glass in the door."

Fear gripped James. "Just be quiet. Both of you. He doesn't know you're there."

"My car's right out front!"

For once, the kid had parked in plain sight instead of getting the lay of the land. "Don't talk unless you see him face-to-face." James pulled up in front of the duplex, threw open the car door and rushed around the side of the house to the backyard, slowing down to tiptoe up the stairs. "I'm putting my phone away. Do not, I repeat, *do not* leave that closet. Whatever happens, let me deal with it. Got it?"

"Yeah," he whispered.

James tucked the phone in his pocket. He debated whether to draw his weapon. Even though Venus insisted, as Baldy also had to the police, that they didn't carry, James couldn't be sure this time. Johnson was looking to save his own life— Venus's testimony could help put him away. Maybe not for life, but for a long time. He was desperate. He had to get her away. He was probably taking her into hiding with him.

He made it to the top stair. He heard the siren then, from a distance, getting louder and closer fast, then a sudden silence. They were there. Backup had arrived.

The door burst open, hitting James dead-on. A short, slender guy shoved him, sending him tumbling. He had a brief sensation of air beneath him, seeing the side of the building flying past, and then he slammed into the ground. Pain shot through him. He tried to move. More pain.

Johnson ran down the steps, tried to leap over him. James caught his leg, yanked it out from under him. He landed facedown. From his scream and the way he grabbed his face, James figured he'd broken his nose. Good, he thought, as two police officers, weapons drawn, came around the corner.

"He's your man," James said. As the world began to tilt, he passed out.

There was a commotion outside James's E.R. curtain.

"You are not stopping me," he heard a woman say. Mysterious. He smiled through his pain-medication-induced euphoria. Then she was there, beside him, her face close to his, tears in her eyes.

"Are you all right?" she demanded.

"Life is good," he said, maybe slurring the words, he wasn't sure, but that was about all that seemed important at the moment. No, there was something.... "I got my priorities straight."

She laid her face against his chest and cried. He patted her back. His hand kept slipping, though. "There, there."

She laughed, a watery kind of sound. "You said you weren't going to get any more scars."

"Do bones get scars? I don't think I lied about that."

Her expression turned solemn. "How can I thank you, Jamey? You were ready to lay down your life for my son."

"My son, too."

Fresh tears sprang to her eyes. She kissed him, the sweetest kiss he'd ever known.

"All right, Mr. Paladin," said the E.R. nurse, swooping in. "Time for a little ride to surgery." She and another aide tugged on his gurney, pulling him out of the curtained cubicle.

"I love you, Caryn," he said as they wheeled him away.

He thought he heard her say she loved him, too, but everything was too hazy. He would let himself think so, anyway, because it would be his last thought before going under. It was a good thought....

James asked that no visitors be allowed into the recovery room. He needed the fog to clear in his head before he talked to Caryn. And Kevin and Venus.

He had no idea what would happen next. Had Caryn said she loved him? He still wasn't sure. But there was still Kevin to deal with. While he'd matured a great deal in a short period of time, James didn't want Kevin to accept him just because he'd helped him out of a jam. Like anyone, James wanted to be accepted for who he was, not for what he'd done.

Later he was taken by wheelchair to the lobby. Caryn, Kevin and Venus stood and hurried toward him. "I rate a parade?" he said, making an effort to set the tone.

Kevin lifted his hand, lowered it, then lifted it again, setting it on James's shoulder. "You okay?"

His touch meant more to James than he could say. His throat closed with happiness. "Yeah. Can we go?"

After some maneuvering, he was situated in the back seat of Caryn's Explorer. Getting up the steps to his house took time and effort as he figured out how to use the crutches. When he finally plopped into his overstuffed chair in the living room, sweat beaded his forehead. He needed to take a pain pill, but he wanted a clear head for the moment. After their necessary conversation he would let himself find oblivion.

"What's going on with your brother?" he asked Venus. Easy stuff first, he decided.

"He's in jail. He says he wasn't going to hurt anyone. He just wanted to get me away."

"Did he admit to taking the money from Caryn?"

Caryn shook her head. "He didn't incriminate himself."

"Do you plan to testify against him?" he asked the younger woman, who looked years older and sad.

"Do I have to?"

"Depends on what you know. How much do you really know?" He was giving her an out. He didn't think she knew much, anyway, not enough to get her brother convicted. Why put her through that?

She locked gazes with him. "Everything I know is speculation."

"What do you want to do, Venus?"

She took a step closer. It was as if they were the only people in the room. "I want to disappear. Like my mom."

"I can help you do that. In fact, I know exactly where to send you."

Hope and relief and doubt crossed her face. "Where?"

"To someone I know. He needs you, too, I think." James pictured the man. Yes, Venus could be very good for him. Might turn his life around. If the bubbly, sweet Venus couldn't do it, he didn't know who could. "You're sure you can leave your past behind?"

"It's not much of a past."

"All right. You'll give your statement to the prosecutors, then we'll arrange a trip for you."

She mouthed a thank-you. After taking another breath she said she would wait in the kitchen for Kevin.

Kevin looked at his mother.

"Would you rather be alone with him?" she asked Kevin.

He shook his head. "I don't think this is the time for secrets."

James smiled. Yes, Kevin had indeed matured.

"Thank you," Kevin said.

"You're welcome." As far as James was concerned, that said it all. They didn't need to rehash it.

"I said some things to you a few days ago," Kevin went on. "Asked you to do something. Asked you to walk away from us."

James didn't look at Caryn, but he heard her quiet intake of breath.

"I take it back," Kevin said.

James's heart opened wide. He forced himself to breathe. "Why?"

"Because everything is different now."

"Why? What's changed? Not out of gratitude, Kevin. I don't want your acceptance out of gratitude."

"I didn't want my mom hurt again. But I heard you tell her you loved her. I don't think you'll hurt her."

"That's enough for you? My loving your mom?" *Give me something more, Kevin.*

Kevin shifted, lowered his head, then looked James in the eye. "What I told you in the beginning was true. I don't need another father. I had a father, and I loved him, no matter what he did. You offered to be my friend…. I think we can start there?"

It was as direct and honest as Kevin could be, James decided.

"I'm willing, Kev."

Kevin leaned down hesitantly and then hugged him. James met Caryn's gaze, saw her smile, saw her eyes mist over.

"I'm going to drive Venus home," Kevin said, then to his mother added, "If you want to stay here and take care of him, I understand."

"I do. Thank you." She hugged him until he couldn't seem to stand it anymore. "I love you."

"Love you, too, Mom."

The front door closed a minute later. Caryn stood where she'd been standing all along. "Can I fix you something to eat or drink?" she asked.

He shook his head, then gestured to the sofa, near him. "Please sit down. You look ready to run."

That was the furthest possible thing from the truth, but she didn't say so. She was nervous, that was all. Not hesitant, not unsure, except of his feelings now that he wasn't under the influence of painkillers and leftover emotion from the situation he'd been in.

She sat. She'd been so scared when Kevin had called her to say James was being taken to the hospital, that he was unconscious. Kevin was almost incomprehensible. His fault, he kept saying. His fault. So stupid. Then when they talked later, while waiting for James's surgery to be done, he told her how it had finally struck him that he was trying to do what Paul and James had done all those years ago—take justice in his own incompetent hands. His guilt over James getting hurt was overwhelming, and a huge lesson to Kevin. They all had to be grateful it wasn't worse.

"Not very talkative, Mysterious?" James asked.

"I don't know where to start."

"No thank-yous, okay?"

She nodded. After fidgeting a moment, she reached for his hand. He grasped hers hard.

"I love you," she said.

He closed his eyes for several long seconds. "I love you, too."

She leaned forward. "I was so scared—"

"Marry me."

"What?"

"Marry me. Tomorrow, next week, whatever. Marry me."

"Jamey, we hardly know each other."

He angled closer, took her face in his hands. "You know it's right. It'll last."

She did. But to act so quickly?

"I want to sleep with you again," he said. "I don't want Kevin to know we didn't wait until the wedding. And I can't wait long, Caryn."

"He's going to wonder why we're in such a hurry. Why we can't at least wait until you're out of your cast."

"So he wonders. So what?" He waited a second. "If you don't kiss me pretty soon—"

She lunged toward him, merged her lips with his, opened her mouth to his, felt the love flow from him, the caring, the ever-after promise in just that one kiss.

"I'll marry you," she said a moment later, her forehead pressed to his. "Do you want children?"

"If it happens, absolutely. I have a story to tell you about that, actually. Later." He grabbed his crutches. "Help me move to the couch so I can hold you."

When she was settled in his arms, she closed her eyes and cherished the moment. "This has to be the strangest connection of all time," she said.

"Yeah. But fated, I think."

"I never would've guess you were a believer in fate."

"There's a lot about me you don't know yet. And vice versa, I figure."

"It'll keep life interesting for a long time."

"Caryn?"

"Hmm?"

"There's room in our love for Paul, too. Always."

Her heart did a slow roll. No wonder she'd fallen in love with him. She thanked him, kissed him and said she loved him again, the first night of countless nights she would tell him that. The first night of the second part of her life. It couldn't get much better than that.

Epilogue

"Pop!"

James angled away from his smoking barbecue grill. The warm October day was as bright and clear as he'd seen. "What, Kev?"

"Look at Emmy."

He shifted his gaze to his just-turned-one-year-old daughter. She'd pulled a tomato from a vine and had taken a huge bite with the six teeth she had. Seeds and juice dripped down her brand-new pink shirt.

James laughed. "Do you want to take charge of the barbecue or your sister?" he asked.

"Barbecue, definitely. Because her diaper needs changing, too." He nudged James out of the way with his hip, grabbing the spatula at the same time.

It was nice having him there for the day. Kevin had

stayed on at the duplex, keeping his independence. It was a good situation.

In the two years since Caryn and James had married, they had become a family, as closely tied as any family that had been together since the beginning, maybe more so because of how they got there.

James wrapped an arm around Kevin's neck and wrestled with him for a second, keeping an eye on the toddler at the same time.

"Emmy!" Caryn exclaimed, coming into the yard.

"Mama," she said, grinning, batting her big turquoise eyes, taking herself out of trouble with the newly learned word. She held out the tomato for Caryn to take a bite.

"Mmm. Warm and sweet, like you, precious," Caryn said, giving her a kiss.

James joined them and took a bite when offered, too.

If this wasn't heaven, he didn't know what was.

"Hey, Pop, I think these burgers are done."

James swallowed. Sometimes moments like this got to him. He was lucky. Damn lucky. He had it all.

He kissed his wife and daughter, picked up the platter of hamburger buns and came up beside his son. Yeah. He had it all.

* * * * *

Silhouette®

Desire®

presents

the final installment of

THREE WAY WAGER

*The Reilly triplets bet they could go
ninety days without sex. Hmm.*

THE LAST
REILLY STANDING
by Maureen Child

(SD #1664, available July 2005)

Aidan Reilly was determined to win the bet
he'd made with his brothers. Three months
without sex meant one thing: spend *a lot* of
time with his best gal pal Terry Evans. She had
given up on love long ago because the pain
just wasn't worth it. Then…temptation proved
to be too much. The last Reilly standing had
lost the bet, but could he win the girl?

Available at your favorite retail outlet.

Welcome to Silhouette Desire's brand-new installment of

*The drama unfolds for six of
the state's wealthiest bachelors.*

BLACK-TIE SEDUCTION
by Cindy Gerard
(Silhouette Desire #1665, July 2005)

LESS-THAN-INNOCENT INVITATION
by Shirley Rogers
(Silhouette Desire #1671, August 2005)

STRICTLY CONFIDENTIAL ATTRACTION
by Brenda Jackson
(Silhouette Desire #1677, September 2005)

*Look for three more titles from Michelle Celmer,
Sara Orwig and Kristi Gold to follow.*

If you enjoyed what you just read,
then we've got an offer you can't resist!

Take 2 bestselling love stories FREE!

Plus get a FREE surprise gift!

Silhouette Desire

Bronwyn Jameson

will take you away with her
breathtaking new miniseries,

PRINCES OF THE OUTBACK

Beginning with

THE RUGGED LONER

Silhouette Desire #1666
Available July 2005

When Angelina Mori returned for the funeral of
Tomas Carlisle's father, offering hugs and tears,
Tomas hadn't felt comforted. He'd dragged in air
rich with her perfume, felt her curves against his
body and set aside this woman who no longer felt
as a childhood friend should. She smelled different,
she looked different and right now, in the dark, he
swore she was looking at him differently, too....

Meet the other Carlisle brothers!
THE RICH STRANGER, available September 2005
THE RUTHLESS GROOM, available November 2005

Only from Silhouette Books!

COMING NEXT MONTH

#1663 BETRAYED BIRTHRIGHT—Sheri WhiteFeather
Dynasties: The Ashtons
When Walker Ashton decided to search for his past, he found it on a
Sioux Nation reservation. Helping him to deal with his Native American
heritage was Tamra Winter Hawk, a woman who cherished her roots
and had Walker longing for a future together. But when his real-world
commitments intruded upon their fantasy liaison, would they find a way
to keep the connection they'd formed?

#1664 THE LAST REILLY STANDING—Maureen Child
Three-Way Wager
Aidan Reilly was determined to win the bet he'd made with his brothers.
Three months without sex meant one thing: spend *a lot* of time with his
best gal pal, Terry Evans. She had given up on love long ago because the
pain just wasn't worth it. Then…temptation proved to be too much. The last
Reilly standing had lost the bet, but could he win the girl?

#1665 BLACK-TIE SEDUCTION—Cindy Gerard
Texas Cattleman's Club: The Secret Diary
Millionaire Jacob Thorne got on Christine Travers's last nerve—the sensible
lady had no time for Jacob's flirtatious demeanor. But when the two butted
heads at an auction, Jacob embarked on a black-tie seduction that would
prove she had needs—womanly needs—that only he could satisfy.

#1666 THE RUGGED LONER—Bronwyn Jameson
Princes of the Outback
Australian widower Tomas Carlisle was stunned to learn he had to father
a child to inherit a cattle empire. Making a deal with longtime friend
Angelina Mori seemed the perfect solution—until their passion escalated
and Angelina mounted an all-out attack on Tomas's defense against hot,
passionate, *committed* love.

#1667 CRAVING BEAUTY—Nalini Singh
They'd married within mere days of meeting. Successful tycoon
Marc Bordeaux had been enchanted by Hira Dazirah's desert beauty. But
Hira feared Marc only craved her outer good looks. This forced Marc to
prove his true feelings to his virgin bride—and tender actions spoke louder
than words….

#1668 LIKE LIGHTNING—Charlene Sands
Although veterinarian Maddie Brooks convinced rancher Trey Walker to
allow her to live and work on his ranch, there was no way Trey would ever
romance the sweet and sexy Maddie. He was a victim of the "Walker Curse"
and couldn't commit to any woman. But once they gave in to temptation,
Maddie was determined to make their arrangement more permanent.…

SDCNM0605